✦ THE ✦
GRAVE ROBBER'S
✦ APPRENTICE ✦

✦ THE ✦ GRAVE ROBBER'S ✦ APPRENTICE ✦

ALLAN STRATTON

SCHOLASTIC INC.

ISBN 978-0-545-60425-3

12 11 10 9 8 7 6 5 4 3 2 1   13 14 15 16 17 18/0

Printed in the U.S.A.   40

First Scholastic printing, September 2013

Typography by Alison Klapthor

For Mom,
who took me to the Stratford Shakespeare Festival
when I was a kid

And for Daniel, Louise, and Christine,
my loyal first readers and friends

TABLE OF CONTENTS

ACT I *The "Little" Countess*

ACT II *The Wolf King*

ACT III *Peter the Hermit*

ACT IV *The Circus of Dancing Bears*

ACT V *Johannes, Prince of Waldland*

ACT I

The "Little" Countess

1

THE BOY IN THE WOODEN CHEST

Years ago, in the Archduchy of Waldland, on a
night when the wind was strong and the waves
were high, a boy washed ashore in a small wooden chest.
The chest took refuge in a nest of boulders at the foot of a
cliff. It swayed there for hours as the surf crashed on either
side, threatening to sweep it away to be gobbled by the deep.

The boy in the chest was a babe, scarce a year old. He
wore a white linen cap and nightshirt, and was bundled tight
in a fine woolen blanket. The sound of the waves was a comfort to him after the screams he'd heard before the chest had
been sealed. Now, as the surf threatened to destroy him, the
infant dreamed he was rocking in his crib.

Meanwhile, up the coast, a stumpy man of lumps and bumps stuck his shovel in the sand and cursed to heaven. It was the grave robber, Knobbe the Bent.

Knobbe plied his trade in County Schwanenberg, in the archduchy's eastern reaches. Tonight, the raging wind had promised a shipwreck—two or three, God willing— so Knobbe had scrambled down the steep cliff path to the beach, hoping to plunder the bodies of the drowned. For hours, he'd prowled the coast, checking the spots where the tide deposited its gifts. He'd found nothing. Not a single corpse. Not even a skeleton dislodged from the seabed, its bony hands still covered in rings.

Knobbe cursed and scratched behind his ear, dislodging a beetle from his matted hair. He began the trek home to his cave, but at the foot of the cliff path he stopped. What was that sparkling in the moonlight? His heart danced up his throat: It was an oak chest, bobbing in a cluster of boulders, the sides inlaid with teak, the lid studded with jewels!

The grave robber dragged the chest to higher ground and pried off the lock with his shovel. Inside, he saw a rich woolen blanket wrapped around some hidden prize. He unspooled the wrapping, hoping to find treasure—perhaps a carved ostrich egg or an ivory horn encrusted with gold. Instead, he came face-to-face with the baby.

Knobbe screamed in shock and tossed the baby in the air. It landed on the sand and started to wail.

"Shut your yap," the grave robber hollered. "It's me what should be crying."

He consoled himself with small mercies. The blanket would keep him warm; the jewels on the chest could be pawned; and the chest itself could be used to stash loot. The baby was another matter. Maybe it could fetch a reward?

Moonlight rippled off the waves and the wet limestone cliffs, revealing a carved crest on the inside of the lid: An eagle's head spewed lightning bolts above two unicorns dancing on a bed of wreaths. Zephyrs blew from the left. The sun shone from the right. A few Latin words scooped the bottom.

Knobbe grunted. The crest was not from the Archduchy of Waldland. The boy was from far away. There would be no reward. Best to leave him on the sand where he lay, then. After all, what good was a baby?

The grave robber made a knapsack with the blanket, put the chest inside, and swung it over his shoulder. "Farewell," he said to the infant.

The boy had stopped crying. He looked up at Knobbe with big solemn eyes.

"Don't play your baby tricks on me," Knobbe warned. "Your sort are all alike. Sneaky little schemers, out to make a fellow weak."

The infant crawled toward him.

"Don't come crawling to me, neither. If you want to beg,

beg to them what locked you in that box and tossed you into the sea."

The infant continued his advance.

Knobbe retreated. "Stay back! I'll take my shovel to you!"

The infant gurgled.

"So I'm funny, am I? Good night to you then!" Knobbe horked a great gob, turned on his heel, and began the long climb home.

Halfway up the cliff, he stopped, leaned against the rock face, thumped the ribs over his heart, and gasped for air. What would become of him when the years piled a weight on his shoulders more crushing than stone?

It was then that a thought emerged, as a ghost ship out of the fog—a thought that caused the grave robber to look down at the tiny creature who'd wriggled his way to the base of the path.

In no time, the brat will be walking, talking, Knobbe thought. *He could be my lookout. A few years more, he'll be able to dig and tunnel and cart my gear. Then, in my old age, he can tend me.*

He'd have to raise the lad, but what of that? A strip of weasel or rat meat would do for feed.

Knobbe descended the cliff. The infant was laughing in wonder, now, at the glittering crabs that skittered from the rocks and sand holes to the sea.

"You, boy, you're mine," the grave robber said. "From this day forth, you're to obey me. Your name shall be Hans, a name as simple and unimportant as you yourself. Understood?"

He hoisted the baby up by its armpits. On its right shoulder was a little birthmark shaped like an eagle. Damaged goods, oh well, who was he to complain? Knobbe plopped the boy into the chest, and hauled him up the cliff to his cave. He had himself a son. And the infant Hans had found a new life as the grave robber's apprentice.

2

GROWING UP GRAVE ROBBING

*H*ans and Knobbe were hunched at the fire pit outside their cave watching the sun go down. Knobbe scratched his bald spot.

"It's over twelve years since you washed up," he said. "Counting your baby time, that makes you thirteen or thereabouts. Think of it. You're all of your fingers and some of your toes." Knobbe had never been to school, but he knew how to count. At least up to twenty.

"How old are you?" Hans asked cautiously.

"Older than all the hairs in my nose. But don't you go changing the subject."

Hans closed his eyes. When Knobbe was fixed on a

subject, he was like a vulture circling a dead rabbit. There was no distracting him till he'd picked the subject clean. But what exactly *was* the subject? Hans nervously traced the little birthmark on his shoulder, waiting for the grave robber's thoughts to land.

Knobbe wormed a string of old squirrel meat from between his teeth. He stared at it gravely. "I've been a good father to you." It was what Knobbe always said when he wanted something.

"Yes, Papa. If it weren't for you I'd have been ripped apart by seagulls." It was what Hans always said when he didn't want to get smacked on the head.

"I spared you from foxes, too. And from the Necromancer," Knobbe continued. "Oh yes, if it weren't for the rope that tied you to my belt when you was an infant, his little minions, the Weevil gang, would have stolen you whilst I was digging up Herr Blooker's grave. Your brains would've been ground up in the Necromancer's skull pot with a little pumpkin seed and gopher dust. You'd have been turned into a spell for the devil."

"Yes, Papa."

"But most of all, I've given you honors," Knobbe intoned. "Honors that lead to the greatest honor of all: initiation into the Grand Society of Grave Robbers."

What will the honor be tonight? Hans shuddered.

When he was a child, the honors had been easy. Knobbe

had hidden him behind stone slabs in various county churchyards while he dug holes in the ground. Hans' honor was to make a birdcall if he heard someone coming. When Hans had realized there were people in the holes, Knobbe'd told him they were friends of his who'd had a tiring life and gone there to sleep. Hans' new honor was the privilege of staying quiet so he wouldn't wake them.

Hans had asked Knobbe why he dug up his friends if they wanted to sleep.

"It's a game of hide-and-seek," Knobbe'd replied. "They hide in the holes. My job is to find them. When I do, they give me their brass buttons."

And other rewards besides buttons. Hans had discovered these by accident. He'd always wanted to see the inside of Knobbe's bounty box—the chest in which he'd been washed ashore—but Knobbe had made it clear that it was off limits. Still, the chest held mysteries for Hans. Where had he come from? Who were his parents? Did they love him? Miss him? And the greatest mystery of all: Who was he? Who was he, really?

One day, Hans' curiosity had gotten the better of him. While Knobbe was away, he'd opened the chest and stared in wonder at the carved crest on the inside of the lid. He'd run his fingers over the eagle spewing lightning bolts, the unicorns, the winds, the sun, and the strange words. Then he'd rummaged through Knobbe's collection of rings, buckles, broaches, and snuffboxes to see if there were other carvings in the wood. At the bottom of the chest, he'd found a cloth bag. It was filled with gold teeth.

That's when Knobbe'd returned. "What are you doing in my bounty box?"

"Nothing."

Knobbe'd grabbed the chest and hugged it tighter than he'd ever hugged his son. "This bounty box holds presents promised me by my friends when they was alive. They're things the dead owe me."

"Even their gold teeth?"

"Especially their gold teeth. They're all I have to remember them by."

Once, Hans had suggested his father might sell these presents, especially the jewelry. With the money, they could dress in real clothes instead of burlap sacks, and have a house in town.

"A house in town means neighbors, and neighbors means questions," Knobbe'd replied. "Best to keep to ourselves, selling the pretties one at a time as needs be. Besides"—and here he'd tapped his nose—"you wouldn't want someone spotting their family's rings on other people's fingers, would you? Pretties must be kept till those who remember them are underground."

"But Papa—"

Knobbe'd held up a hand. "There are things you're too

11

young to understand, my boy. Things you'll know when you enter the Grand Society of Grave Robbers."

As Hans grew into a wiry young man, the "little honors" his father bestowed on him had become more physical. After years of digging in the damp, stony earth, Knobbe's right shoulder had ballooned like a pumpkin, while the bunions on his large, hairy feet bulged unto bursting. So Hans was obliged to carry shovels, ropes, and crowbars, and to dig down till he tapped a coffin. Then he'd scramble out of the hole, leaving Knobbe to deal with the dead.

Yet crawling in and out of graves was getting harder on the old man's bones. Thus, tonight, Hans was not entirely surprised to hear his latest honor:

"In three nights' time, there'll be a new moon," said Knobbe. "On that night, you shall rob your very first grave single-handed, and enter the Grand Society of Grave Robbers."

Hans felt sick. Knobbe was blessed with a weak nose and a strong stomach; Hans was not. When the grave robber toiled in the holes, Hans closed his eyes and dreamed of daylight, birdsong, and the roar of the sea. He couldn't condemn the man who'd saved his life and raised him since childhood. Yet the idea that in three days he'd be robbing a grave himself was unbearable.

Knobbe smacked Hans on the side of the head. "What's the matter? I offer you the greatest honor of your life, and not a word of thanks?"

"I'm sorry, Papa." From the corner of his eye, Hans saw a turkey vulture glide past the cliff edge and over the sea. It hovered, then swooped through the dusk toward the distant turrets on Castle Hill. *Oh, to be a bird, to soar free, high above the earth,* Hans thought. *Oh, to be anywhere but here.*

He rose unsteadily to his feet.

"What is it, boy?" Knobbe growled.

"It's . . . I'm . . . It's . . ." Hans swallowed and swallowed and swallowed. His arms circled limply at his sides.

"Spit it out."

Hans could barely hear or think or breathe. It was as if he was underwater, drowning. His feet began to move, all on their own, one in front of the other.

"Where are you off to?"

Hans neither knew nor cared. He swayed to the crag beyond the fire pit and started to run, bounding out of the barrens and into the gathering night. On and on he ran, through Potter's Field, past the churchyard, into the village, his bare feet pounding the cobblestones outside the baker's, the blacksmith's, the tinker's, the tailor's, and over the bridge by the mill. Back in the country, guided by starlight, he turned off the road, jumped over a ditch, and tore through fields and groves till he could run no more. He dropped to his knees by a stand of bulrushes at the foot of Castle Hill.

Hans froze. He'd crossed into the estate of the Count and Countess von Schwanenberg and of their daughter, Angela, the Little Countess. If he were caught, there'd be trouble. Yet Hans was powerless to move. He could only gaze up in wonder at the castle above him. From the barrens, it looked impressive. Here, so close, it seemed a miracle of God.

Hans lay on his side and imagined life within its gilded walls. How glorious it must be for even the lowliest of the lowliest servants. Maybe they had to empty chamber pots and clean out the stables, but at least they never had to rob graves.

Hans made a promise to the stars: "One day, I shall know who I am. From that day forth, I shall live in the light, breathe clean air, and never again have to crawl with the dead things." Then his eyelids flickered shut and he drifted into a sleep far deeper and more troubled than the grave.

3

THE "LITTLE" COUNTESS

"**P**repare to die, Boy!" howled the Necromancer. "I'll drain your blood to feed my ghouls!"

The Boy hung from a hook on the back wall, his wooden head and limbs smudged with dirt and clay. A line of hideous creatures, suspended by strings, scraped toward him. Out of the dark a voice rang out: "Halt, O Specters of Hell! It is I, Angela Gabriela, Avenger of God!"

The line of ghouls stopped in its tracks. The Necromancer trembled. Angela Gabriela was about to swoop in, wielding her Sword of Justice.

Only she didn't. She was distracted by a snore—a screechy snore as loud as a hog at market that echoed around

15

the little turret theater.

The Countess Angela Gabriela von Schwanenberg had had enough. She stormed from her perch above the puppet stage and marched through the side curtains to confront her audience, the Necromancer marionette swinging from her right hand.

The usual suspects were in attendance, propped up on a row of mismatched castle chairs: Lord Forgetful, Lady Bottoms-Up, Mistress Tosspot, and General Confusion. Angela knew they were innocent. After all, they were nothing but pillows and cushions sewn together and draped in costume finery, with button eyes and horsehair wigs. The fifth audience member was another matter altogether.

"Nurse!" Angela exclaimed. "Nurse!"

Nurse blinked in midsnore. Seeing Angela, she clapped wildly. "Bravo, Little Countess! Bravo!"

"Stop calling me 'Little' Countess. I'm twelve. In barely a month, thirteen!"

Nurse pursed her lips, adjusted her spectacles, and took up her knitting, an endless gray shawl that had fallen from her ample lap onto her sewing basket. "Oh my!" she muttered, so Angela could hear. "A full grown-up countess still playing with her dollies."

Angela flushed. "They aren't dollies, they're marionettes. And if you don't stop ruining this rehearsal, next week's production will be a disaster. Please, Nurse. Mother and Father will be coming. I need them to like it. I want to make them proud."

"Then do a lute duet with the music master. That would be far more ladylike."

Angela bristled. "Puppet troupes are serious business. They perform at all the great courts of Europe."

Nurse glanced heavenward. "Aren't we a little big for our petticoats? Here you are in a child's nursery, talking about the great courts of Europe."

"My theater is not a nursery! Father imported it from Venice. The curtains are velvet. The stage is oak."

"Indeed," Nurse mocked. "And the audience is stuffed with goose feathers." She winked at the pillow-head slumped to her right. "Isn't that right, Lord Forgetful? You're not quite up for a ball at the palace, are you?"

"Be as mean as you like," Angela said. "Plays matter."

Nurse snorted and took a gander at Angela's newest creation. The marionette's body was wrapped in a dirty velvet shroud. The arms and legs sticking out from it were goose bones. The head was an owl's skull, its eye sockets empty.

"What fiendish thing is this?" Nurse whispered.

"If you bothered to watch my rehearsals, you'd know," Angela said, barely hiding her hurt and fury.

Nurse clutched her chest. "I asked you a question. What have you made? What have you done?"

"I've made the Necromancer, as if it isn't obvious. See

the bits of dried leaves I glued to the bones to look like his scaly skin?"

"That doll of yours will summon the creature himself," Nurse trembled. "He'll sweep up from his lair in Potter's Field, him and his crows. He'll enter your dreams. He'll ruin us."

"For heaven's sake, Nurse," Angela sighed, "if the Necromancer could really speak to the dead and make evil spells, Father would do something."

"Even your father dares not touch him," Nurse said. "Oh, Angela, his power is real. Ask anyone in the village. Destroy that thing!"

"No!"

"Then I shall!" Nurse exclaimed, and grabbed the puppet in both hands. Angela darted about her, screaming to get it back, but Nurse was on a mission. She dashed the owl skull on the stone floor, broke the goose bones across her knee, and wrapped the shards in the velvet shroud.

"You had no right to destroy my puppet," Angela cried. "I am the Countess Angela Gabriela von Schwanenberg!" She tossed her golden curls in fury and strode to the turret window, chin up, chest out.

"A countess doesn't sulk," Nurse said.

"I'm not sulking," Angela snapped. "This is an intermission."

"Is it now?" Nurse removed the crucifix from her

18

neck and tied it tight around the unholy bundle. Then she returned to her chair, placed the broken puppet in the bottom of her sewing basket, and laid her knitting on top.

Angela gazed out the turret window to the barrens on the horizon. All she cared about was her theater, but Nurse was right. It was a nursery. Despite her titles she was a child, a girl, a nothing. Her future? To marry some stranger and be stuck in his castle far from home. Her only pretending would be pretending to be happy.

As if she wasn't pretending to be happy now. *I'm all alone, except for my puppets*, she thought. *Mother and Father haven't time for me, and who can I play with? No one.*

It was true. An only child of noble birth, she could hardly mingle with the village urchins, and the offspring of other counts lived so far away they might as well be dreams. Except for Georgina von Hoffen-Toffen, who'd been a nightmare. She'd mocked Angela's theater and called her silly. Then she'd married Archduke Arnulf and drowned in a bath of milk. So now who was silly?

Angela sniffed and turned her gaze north to the sunny farms that led to the great forest and the far mountains beyond. She thought of the ghost marionette she'd made of Georgina, and of the others. The one of herself, of course, and of the Necromancer, and of the strange, mysterious Boy from the barrens. He starred in all her plays. Sometimes he was a rogue, other times a wretch or a hero who'd save her from the Wolf King, said to live in the great forest with his monster horde. Nurse had noticed Angela's interest in the Boy. She called it unnatural. Then again, Nurse found everything unnatural except for her Bible and her knitting.

Still, why did Angela think of the Boy? He was a peasant—a nobody—with hair as brown as dirt and a pale complexion ruddied by clay. He stood alone in ditches when her family's carriage passed by, or at the edge of the village square on feast days. Angela imagined she'd need a perfumed handkerchief over her nose to get within ten feet of him. Yet when he glanced at her, she always blushed and looked away.

Angela gasped. No sooner had the Boy crossed her mind than her eyes had drifted to the bulrushes at the foot of Castle Hill—and there he was, asleep. *How wonderful to come and go as one pleases*, she thought. *How wonderful to be free.*

But what was he doing on her estate? Should she call the guards? If he were caught, he'd be in trouble. But if he was up to no good and she did nothing, whatever he did would be her fault. What was he in real life: hero or villain?

"What are you looking at?" said Nurse.

"Nothing," Angela fluttered. "It's time to get back to the rehearsal."

"Not so fast, my girl." Nurse had a nose for mischief, and it was twitching up a storm. She made her way to the window, propped herself against the casement, and had a good squint. "God spare us!"

"From what? He hasn't done anything."

"Oh, but he will, my love!" Nurse pointed to the county road.

It was then that Angela realized Nurse wasn't frightened of the Boy. She was terrified at the sight of the twenty soldiers galloping toward the castle. In their lead, a team of stallions drew a fearful black carriage. It bore the standard of His Royal Highness Archduke Arnulf, ruler absolute of the Archduchy of Waldland.

4

PRISONERS

*T*he archduke's troops tore into the courtyard, leaped from their horses, and stormed the entrance hall. Angela heard a torrent of noise below—her parents' cries, the servants' prayers, and a clang of armor bounding up the stairs. She ran to Nurse for protection as four soldiers burst in. One tossed Nurse to the ground. Another, the size of a house, hoisted Angela over his shoulder.

"Put me down," she shrieked. "I'm Countess Angela Gabriela von Schwanenberg."

The soldier laughed and whisked her to the staircase. Angela pounded his back, bruising her hands on his heavy chain mail. "My father will have you in irons."

The soldier knocked her against the wall like a sack of potatoes. Angela tried to bite his ear, but got only a mouthful of helmet and hair. Descending into a blur of confusion, she saw maids and valets herded into a circle by six of the archduke's men.

Next thing she knew, she was being carried across the courtyard to a carriage with bars on the windows. The soldier swung open the door and tossed her inside. She landed hard on a wooden bench. Her parents were seated opposite. Angela wanted to throw herself in their arms, but she was afraid to shame the family.

"Chin up," her father said tightly.

"All will be well," her mother echoed.

The driver cracked his whip. The archduke's horses reared with a fierce bray and flew down Castle Hill. Angela peered between the bars and watched her home disappear in a whirlwind of colors and dust.

"What's going on?" she asked, struggling to control her voice. "Where's the archduke?"

"He's with the archduchess at his palace," her father replied, as if everything was normal. "We've been summoned for an audience. The soldiers are escorting us."

"Has Nurse been taken too?"

"I believe we're His Highness' only guests," her mother said.

"Guests?"

"Yes," her mother said discreetly. She fanned herself. "An invitation to the palace is a great honor. Don't fret. Nurse will attend to things while we're away."

Angela looked from one to the other as if they'd gone crazy. That's when she saw her father's knuckles pressing up through his silk gloves and the lines on her mother's face breaking through her powder, and realized her parents were as frightened as she was. They had no idea what was happening either and, whatever it was, no power to stop it. It was the first time she'd ever seen them helpless, and it scared her to death.

There followed a hard, three-day ride to the archduke's palace in the capital. The carriage followed the coast. It stormed up rugged cliffs, hurtled along craggy beaches, and rattled over perilous bridges spanning rivers and steep ravines. Between the window bars on the left, Angela glimpsed the brilliant blues and whitecaps of the sea. To the right, she saw fields and woods sweeping north to the far mountains.

The soldiers paused to change horses at various of the archduke's country stables, stationed at intervals along the way. During these stops, they poked a little dry bread and cheese through the bars for food.

The count and countess wilted faster than cut flowers. By first nightfall, they'd loosened the heavy satin ruffles at their throats. By dawn, they were using the ruffles to wipe their sweat. And then, dear Lord, they took off their wigs. Angela had never seen her mother's hair before—a close-cropped gray—or known that her father was bald. It was a shocking sight, like seeing them naked.

She looked away. When she looked back, she caught them staring at her with longing and regret. Her mother inched her fingers forward, and instantly pulled them back.

"Mother?"

"I was just wondering . . . ," her mother said awkwardly. "That is, I wasn't sure . . . but if it would please you . . . would you like me to hold you?"

Angela hesitated. "I'm not sure. I'm almost thirteen. Would it be all right?"

"I think so. Yes," her mother said. In a heartbeat, Angela was pressed to her chest. She was glad there was no one to see. Especially Nurse.

Her father cleared his throat. "We could tell stories. That would pass the time." He stroked a damp ringlet from Angela's forehead. "You'd planned a puppet play for us, I think. Tell us about it. Your stories are always so good."

"Do you mean it?" Angela asked. "You like them?"

"Of course," her mother said in wonder. "Didn't you know?"

Angela shook her head.

"Oh, my darling."

In no time, Angela was acting out her entire play.

Her forefinger shrouded in a handkerchief became the Necromancer. Her little finger, the Boy. The role of Herself was played by a thumb. She thrilled as her parents cheered and applauded and praised her more than they ever had at the castle.

Angela closed her eyes and for a moment the carriage prison disappeared. She'd always wondered if her parents loved her. Now, she not only knew it, she *felt* it. And she knew that she loved them back, and always would, more than anything in the world.

THE PALACE

*L*ate on the third and final day of the journey, Angela became aware of a strange mist in the air. At first it came in wisps so light and delicate they vanished almost before they were seen. But soon the mist became bold— thick fingers of fog that swirled into tentacles. They wrapped around the carriage and snaked between the window bars. Color and light were smothered in gray.

In no time, all Angela could see were the ghostly shapes of things floating out of the gloom: trees and barns, then tumbledown buildings as the carriage left the country- side. Now, instead of thundering on dirt roads, the horses' hooves clattered on city cobblestones.

"It's the capital, Nebelstad," her father said. "Archduke Arnulf's palace is near."

The family fell silent. The count and countess fumbled to restore their wigs and ruffles.

They passed the port. Angela heard a wash of gulls, fog-horns, bells, and tavern songs and saw the silhouettes of ships and wharves and men unloading crates and livestock. When the men saw the archduke's soldiers, they dropped everything and fled.

The carriage turned away from the port and entered the city's Old Town. The narrow streets wound in all directions. Oil lamps lit the way, globes of sooty yellow swimming in the dark. *Where are the people?* Angela wondered. It was as if the world was hiding.

At last the street opened into a public square lined with grand buildings. Angela pictured it by day, a farmers' market filled with stalls overflowing with fruits and vegetables, a place alive with gossip and barter, with minstrels and acro-bats. Now it was dead as Potter's Field. Lamps and torches threw shadows through the mist; they danced and disap-peared like spirits.

"That's the Cathedral of Saint Simeon," her father said quietly as they passed a domed edifice to their right. "Its catacombs stretch all the way under Market Square to the palace."

"What's that?" Angela asked, pointing in awe to a

majestic pillar. Ornamental steps circled to the top, where three marble coffins lay under an open canopy of wrought iron.

"It's the monument to Arnulf's brother, the good Archduke Fredrick, his wife, and their infant son," her mother said. "She died in childbirth. Fredrick and his son were killed when pirates attacked their ship. Had they lived, Arnulf would never have been crowned. What a better world it would've been."

"Hush," her father whispered. "Do you want us to lose our tongues?"

The carriage swooped left and came to a sudden halt.

"We've arrived." Her mother pinched her cheeks, as if a blush could erase the hardship of the journey.

Soldiers unlocked the doors. Angela crawled out slowly. Her legs wobbled. She gripped a carriage wheel for support. It wasn't the journey's jostle and cramp that made her weak, but the sight of the palace. Angela looked up and up and up. Spires, turrets, and parapets soared into the night. From each of them, gargoyles—winged, horned, and clawed—glared down, ready to pounce.

Angela heard wails rising from the grates at her feet. "Where do those sounds come from?" she whispered to her mother.

"The dungeon," her mother murmured.

The screams gave way to the squeal of the bronze doors

of the palace. Twice the height of a man, they swung open, pushed by a dozen servants in dark velvet livery.

A gnomelike gentleman advanced from the vaulted entry hall. He had a protruding forehead and chin that made his face look like the inside of a spoon. "His Royal Highness Archduke Arnulf is attending to the archduchess," the Spoon said. "You shall be received in the morning. Now, follow me to your quarters."

The Spoon led them up three flights of stairs and along an eternity of corridors. At length they came to a hall lined with suits of armor. Between each suit was a bedchamber locked with a heavy bolt.

"This is your room," the Spoon said to Angela's parents. "Your daughter shall be down the hall."

"Surely you don't mean to separate us," her mother pleaded.

"It's all right," Angela said. "I'm perfectly fine." She wasn't, of course, but she wanted to spare her parents worry.

Her room was spacious, if spare: a canopied bed, a desk with a stool and oil lamp, and a rocking chair with broad armrests. A fresh cotton nightdress with embroidered wildflowers and lace trim lay across the goose-down duvet. *What a shame to be dirty in such a pretty dress*, Angela thought.

No sooner had the thought of her filth crossed her mind than a big-boned housekeeper rolled in a copper tub full of steaming hot water scented with jasmine, lavender, and rose petals. Angela quickly removed her clothes, except for her underthings. She'd never been shy, but there was something about the room she didn't trust: the full-length painting of *The Devil Greets the Maiden* on the far wall. She had the odd feeling that the devil in the painting was staring at her.

After the bath, the housekeeper wrapped her in a thick towel, wrung her hair, and brushed it. "Shall I prepare you for bed?" she asked, holding up the nightdress.

Angela gave the painting a suspicious look. "A moment, if you please, Housekeeper." She took the nightie, got onto her mattress, and drew the canopy curtains shut. Only then did she wriggle out of her wet undergarments and change into her nightdress. Venturing forth, she knelt to say her prayers, taking the opportunity to peek under the bed. There was nothing but three dust balls and a mouse pellet.

She crawled under the duvet. "Please leave the canopy curtains closed," she said. "I won't be able to sleep with the devil watching me."

Snug in her tent of draperies, Angela listened as the housekeeper rolled the copper tub out into the corridor and returned for the oil lamp. The light seemed to float through the air. It was all quite magical until the door was bolted shut and the room cast into utter darkness.

6

DIGGING UP YORICK

*B*ack on the barrens, Hans prepared for his own night of horror. It was the new moon, the time that Knobbe had decreed he must rob his first grave.

Three days earlier, Hans had woken to the sight of the royal carriage galloping up Castle Hill. He'd snuck home to the cave, racked with guilt. *It's a terrible thing to steal from the dead,* he'd thought, *but how can I abandon Papa? He saved my life.* When Hans had begged forgiveness, the grave robber'd grunted, "If it's forgiveness you want, do my feet. They've swelled up fierce." Hans had rubbed the bloated pads and Knobbe had welcomed him home.

Now Hans wondered if maybe he should've stayed away

after all. Within the hour he'd be stripping a corpse of its rings and boots, its glasses and teeth. He'd be touching decayed flesh; feeling the damp where the rot oozed.

He swallowed hard and watched as Knobbe tossed on the old monk's robe he'd stolen from an abbey. The robe had a large hood that covered his head and hid the rat scar on his cheek. Knobbe considered it a perfect disguise. Hans wasn't so sure. He figured anyone would be curious to see a monk with a shovel standing over a corpse in an open grave.

Knobbe glanced over. "What are you staring at, lazy-bones?"

"Nothing." Hans looped a rope around his shoulder and picked up his wooden shovel. His hands sweat so much it nearly slid from his grip.

"What's wrong with you?" Knobbe demanded. "You're about to strip your very first coffin. Show some enthusi-asm."

Hans closed his eyes and tried to imagine birdsongs. "I'm ready."

"Then we're off." Knobbe raised a lantern and guided them into the dark. "Your task tonight is a good deed for a widow in need," he said as they crossed the barrens. "You remember Yorick Grimwort, the scoundrel who gambled his fortune and left his poor wife to pay his debts?"

Hans nodded glumly.

"Well, the widow Grimwort was no fool," Knobbe

confided. "Before the bailiffs could claim her valuables, she sewed them in his stomach. He was buried full of coins and cutlery. Now the widow's begged a favor: that I might fetch them back in exchange for some of the pretties. Returning the poor woman's treasures is the least the good Lord would have us do."

Yorick Grimwort was planted with the damned in the unholy ground of Potter's Field, a vast boneyard that stretched beyond the iron gates of the village church. It was an awful, lonely place. Aside from a whistle of wind, the only sounds were the whispers of villagers seeking the Necromancer for a spell and the scurry of his Weevil gang lurking in the tall grass.

Hans and Knobbe gingerly made their way across the pitted terrain of brambles, weed, and rock. Every so often they passed a grave marked by a brick. Most often, though, the only marker was a hollow in the ground where the coffin below had collapsed. *How awful to be alone and forgotten*, Hans thought.

They arrived at Yorick's resting place. Hans' cheeks went pale as the moon. He began to dig, his insides churning with every shovel of earth. At last he reached the coffin. He closed his eyes and pictured himself as a bird flying high and free in the fresh air. Then he took a deep breath and pried open the lid.

In life, Yorick Grimwort had smelled of old fish guts.

Death hadn't improved matters. Hans wriggled a rag from his pocket and pressed it over his nose. He opened his eyes. At that very moment, a beetle crawled out of Yorick's left nostril and waved its antennae. Hans promptly heaved.

"In the name of the Great Himself!" Knobbe exclaimed. "There's no need to make the job disgusting. Where's your respect for the dead?"

"I'm sorry," Hans said as he scrambled out of the grave.

Knobbe cursed, eased down into the hole, and straddled the corpse. He lifted Yorick's tunic and tugged at the cord the widow Grimwort had sewn across her husband's belly. The stitch fell away. Knobbe pulled out coins and cutlery like stuffing from a turkey. But when he hauled the loot up from the hole, a spasm seared his lower back.

"Aaa!" He lurched his head toward Hans. "Useless wretch. You're the cause of my pain. Rob a grave by month's end, or I'll cast you out. Now go!"

Hans ran from Potter's Field, the words burning in his ears. He'd never be able to steal from the dead. So how could he gain his father's love?

Once more, he ended up at the stand of bulrushes at the foot of Castle Hill. Lanterns lit the gates above. Torches glowed from the halls beyond the windows. Lamplight twinkled like stars from the upper parapets. The castle appeared to be resting, peaceful and happy, awaiting the return of its noble family.

Hans remembered his glimpse of the royal coach. How wonderful it must have been for the Little Countess to ride to the palace in that magnificent carriage. How exciting to be the guests of the archduke himself. What a thrill to have all those soldiers at their command.

Hans wished he could be so lucky.

THE MIDNIGHT VISITOR

*A*ngela shivered under her duvet. It was barely two minutes since the housekeeper had locked her in the pitch-black cell, and already she was petrified.

She told herself it was because tonight was her first night away from home and that the sounds on the other side of the bed curtains didn't exist: such as the sound of things wriggling across the floor, and scratching against the woodwork, and scuttling up and down inside the walls.

It's only mice, she thought, and instantly pictured the rodents climbing up the bed legs, and crawling under the duvet. She imagined that every tickle and itch was whiskers and every draft the fluttering of bats in the canopy over her head.

Finally exhaustion overcame her and she fell asleep. At least she hoped she fell asleep, because what happened next was too terrifying to be true.

In her nightmare, Angela roused to hear something peculiar happening at the painting of *The Devil Greets the Maiden*. Someone or something was stepping down from the canvas onto the floor. The boards creaked. Footsteps crept toward her bed. The brass rings on the curtain rod rattled gently. The drapery parted.

Angela felt a weight on the edge of the mattress. She froze as the creature slid onto the bed. It wormed its way beside her. Its hand brushed against her cheek and stroked her forehead. Its fingers were cold and clammy.

"Angela Gabriela von Schwanenberg," it said in the voice of a young woman.

"Who are you?" Angela quivered. "*What* are you?"

"I am the archduchess."

Angela's nurse had warned her that the devil takes many forms. To come as an archduchess was surely clever. "How do you know my name?"

"You are the one that he sent for. You are my death."

Angela shivered. "What do you mean?"

"I've come to warn you. He will wait till your thirteenth birthday, as he waited for mine. But once he has your dowry, he will seek another and you will be done for."

"Who'll have my dowry?" Angela asked. "Who'll seek another?"

"My husband. Archduke Arnulf. The one who seeks my death even as we speak."

"I don't believe you," Angela shuddered. "You're the fiend come to haunt my dreams!"

"Does this feel like a dream?"

"No, but the worst nightmares always seem real. I'm going to wake myself up, and when I do, you'll disappear."

The devil laughed the laugh of a madwoman. "I didn't trust the last archduchess when she came to me either. Georgina. They say she fell asleep in a bath of milk. It's a lie. My husband drowned her."

There were shouts from the corridor.

"Farewell," her visitor said. "Pray I survive the night."

Angela heard a fumbling with the bolt. The door to the room was thrown open. The housekeeper stormed in, followed by two soldiers. "Where is she?" she thundered.

"Who?"

"You know perfectly well."

"I don't," Angela gasped, heart pounding. "I'm alone. I had a nightmare. The devil told me my friend, Georgina, was murdered."

The housekeeper gave her a hard look and checked under the bed. "Nothing," she growled to the guards. "The rest of the night, I watch from the rocker!"

Angela fell back on her pillow. She glanced at the painting on the wall. The devil looked down at her. He seemed to be smiling.

A DEADLY PROPOSAL

ngela was awake the rest of the night. Had the visitation been a dream? Was it a trick of the devil? Or had the archduchess really come to her, perhaps by means of some secret passageway behind the painting? Angela prayed it was a dream or the devil. If it were the archduchess, she'd be too scared to ever sleep again.

At dawn, maidservants brought her new clothes: a pale yellow frock adorned with a rich brocade about the bodice, a matching bonnet, white silk stockings and undergarments, an ivory fan, and satin shoes with silver buckles. Angela dressed quickly and soon was reunited with her parents. They were likewise in fresh attire, with elaborate new wigs. Her father's had three large rolls above each ear; her mother's was in the shape of a ship. It was as if they'd been costumed for a fancy dress ball.

What cruel sport is this? Angela wondered.

Her mother held her. "Thank heaven you're safe."

Her father kissed her forehead. "We were alarmed by all the shouting."

"Much ado about nothing," Angela smiled. Her playacting calmed them.

A bell tinkled. The Spoon appeared. "His Royal Highness Archduke Arnulf is ready to see you." He escorted Angela and her parents to the throne room, a hall so vast and dark that its vaulted ceiling and rear alcoves seemed to disappear into night.

Angela shrank. All around, the mounted heads of stags, bears, and wolves stared down at her. Ahead, she could dimly see an oak table covered in parchments with archducal seals, a globe, and the throne itself, an ebony marvel alive with carved dragons. Beside the throne was a matching stool with a red satin cushion; at its center was a small gold statue on a chain, depicting a pair of hands clasped in prayer.

"Friends," said Archduke Arnulf, emerging from the shadows in a military breastplate and armored hands, arms, and legs.

Angela and her parents fell to the floor.

"Rise," he commanded. "How good to see my loyal subjects, the Count and Countess von Schwanenberg." He turned to Angela. "And you must be the Little Countess, Angela Gabriela."

Angela curtsied twice. "Your Highness."

She couldn't help noticing that the archduke looked nothing like his official portrait, which hung in the dining hall of every noble family in the archduchy. The portrait featured a dashing young man, lean of body, ruddy of cheek, but Arnulf in the flesh was another creation. His frame was as stout as a wine barrel, his hair as long and murky as a basket of river snakes, and his face as pale as dawn, with thin blue lips and a rim of red under the eyes. A large, purple vein pulsed at his left temple.

"I trust you had a good sleep?" the archduke inquired.

Her parents looked down. "Yes, Your Highness."

He turned to Angela. "And you?"

"I slept soundly, Your Highness."

Arnulf chuckled. "You're an excellent actress, Little Countess, much better than your parents. But I'm told you had a fearsome dream." He cupped her chin in an armored paw. "Don't try to fool me. I have eyes everywhere." Angela tried to look away; Arnulf held her fast. "Once more—and this time the truth—tell me about your night."

"If you must know, it was horrible," Angela blurted. "What do you expect? For three days, your soldiers kept my parents and me locked up in a carriage like criminals. Then we were held in pitch-black cells under guard."

The archduke laughed. "A saucy tongue. I like that." He eyed her closely. "Show me your gums." He inspected her teeth as if she were a horse. "A full set. Good," he said. "You'll do well at the palace."

"Your Highness?" the count and countess asked in confusion.

"I'm in need of a new archduchess," Arnulf said. "I seem to have found her."

"But Your Highness already has an archduchess," her father said hoarsely.

"Alas, no more," Archduke Arnulf sighed. "Last night, the poor thing tripped and caught her braids on a doorknob. She strangled on her ribbons."

Angela's head swam. There could be no more pretending. Her visit with the archduchess was real. Her life was in danger.

Her parents sensed danger, too. Spots of crimson flushed her mother's cheeks. Her father's fingers twitched.

"It is a heavy loss, Your Highness," her mother said in her courtliest manner. "Yet, while we are honored by your proposal, surely it is unwise to pick a bride when lost in grief."

The archduke shrugged. "I am in *constant* grief. My wives are no sooner wed than dead. They fall off parapets, tumble down staircases, and go to sleep in their baths. It's why I invited you here while the last clumsy creature was alive. I felt the need to plan ahead." He whispered in Angela's ear: "Promise me *you're* not clumsy."

Angela shook her head in terror.

Her father cleared his throat. "With great respect, our Angela is but a child."

"Not so," the archduke corrected. "In a month, she'll be thirteen. A common enough age to wed."

"Quite," her mother nodded in panic. "Yet in truth," she lied, "our Angela has been promised to the Convent of the Holy Sisters of Schwanenberg. She's to take her vows next Sunday."

Angela gulped. Becoming a nun wasn't the future she'd pictured for herself, but it was certainly better than marriage to a murderous madman.

"The archduchy has more than enough holy sisters," Arnulf yawned. "I'll make a donation to the mother superior. Your daughter will be released from her pledge."

"Thank you," Angela said, surprised by the sound of her own voice. "Even so, I'm afraid I have other dreams than to be an archduchess."

Arnulf raised an eyebrow.

Angela swallowed hard. "I have a puppet theater where I produce plays. It's my fondest wish to perform in the great courts of Europe. So you see, I won't have time for marriage."

"Oh, but you *will*. You shall entertain *my* court each night," Arnulf gurgled. "I love puppets. In fact, I have one of my own. A special marionette." The vein at his temple started to throb. He pressed it gently, then went to the stool with the gold statue of the praying hands. He raised the statue by the chain that ran through its middle fingertips. "A simple puppet on a string. See how I make it frolic." He jerked the chain and the golden hands hopped about.

Angela clapped politely. "What do the hands represent?"

Arnulf winked. "It's not what they represent—it's what they hold. Come see." He held the statue in front of Angela's nose. There was a little crystal window above the cupped thumbs. Through it, Angela saw that the statue held two sets of hand bones.

"They're mine," Arnulf confided.

Angela trembled. "What happened?"

"I had them removed," Arnulf said airily. He hung the chain around his neck. The bones in the reliquary rattled.

"Then what's under your armor?" Angela asked, pointing at his sheathed mitts.

"This is no armor," Arnulf said, his voice as thick as gravy. "These are my *new* hands. My *iron* hands. Observe the movable fingers and joints." He wiggled a wave. "With these I can pen letters. Or attend to more *pressing* matters." He strode to a marble bust beside the middle window. "Behold the head of my brother, the late Archduke

Fredrick." He placed his iron hands on either side of the bust and squeezed. The marble turned to dust.

Jaws dropped.

"I asked the former bishop of the Cathedral of Saint Simeon to bless these hands," the archduke said mildly. "He refused. His body lies with his fellow martyrs in the catacombs. His head, however, sits by my bedside in a reliquary of its own." He paused. "The present bishop respects my wishes. I trust you will too."

Angela's father gathered his courage. "No, Your Highness! You cannot have my daughter!"

Archduke Arnulf grabbed him by the throat. "Yes, Count, I can." He lifted Angela's father off the floor. "Give me your blessing."

"Never," the count choked. His legs flailed the air. He clutched the iron fist.

Angela threw herself at the archduke's feet. "Stop! Spare my father and I'll marry you!"

"Willingly?" Arnulf asked. "An unhappy bride would ruin the celebration."

"I'll be the happiest, willingest bride in all of Christendom!"

Arnulf released his grip. The count fell to the floor. Arnulf rolled him over with a toe. "As for the dowry, Count, you have a fine stable. I shall take it, as well as a gift of ten gold ducats from each of your citizens."

"Ten gold ducats!" the countess exclaimed. "The people can't afford it!"

"Where there's a will, there's a way," the archduke observed, "and I most certainly have the will." He clapped his hands. There was a dreadful echoey clang. "Begone. In one month, I shall meet you at Castle Schwanenberg to take my dowry. Then I shall escort your Angela to the cathedral for her marriage."

9
A GLIMMER OF HOPE

*I*t was a somber ride home from the palace. Angela tried not to stare at her parents, but it was impossible. Her mother trembled like a sparrow in winter, while bruises dark as a string of plums ringed her father's neck.

Suddenly, her father's eyes popped open. Putting his hand to his throat, he whispered into her mother's ear. She brightened instantly.

"Angela," she said. "Do you remember the story of your christening?"

Angela nodded. "You didn't know what to name me, even as we came to the priest. But there was a wise fool in the churchyard, newly arrived in the village."

"Peter the Hermit," her mother said, barely able to contain herself.

"Peter the Hermit, yes."

Angela's father circled his hand for her to go on, as if hope lay in the telling of the tale.

"Peter the Hermit said he could see angels hovering over me," Angela continued. "He said they'd always protect me and keep me safe. That's why you named me Angela Gabriela. Angela for the angels and Gabriela for the archangel Gabriel."

"That's right," her mother said. "Peter was such a kindly man we let him sleep in the castle haymow. After a month he left for the far mountains, where he founded a hermitage for lost souls like himself."

"I know, I know," Angela frowned. "But what has this to do with me?"

"Angela, my love—your father and I shall have you spirited to Peter the Hermit's retreat. Hidden in the mountain clouds, you'll be safe from discovery." Her mother beamed, triumphant. Her father nodded with delight.

Angela looked from one to the other. "What of the servants who'd bring me there? The archduke would torture out their secret and I'd be hunted down and killed. So would the servants, the hermits, and you."

A pall descended, the silence filled by the rattle of the carriage and the clatter of the horses' hooves. Her parents squeezed Angela's hand.

"Angela," her mother said, "despite how things may seem, never give up hope. Hope will see you through the darkest times when those around you are broken by despair." Her face crumpled. She covered it with her fan.

Back at the castle, Angela tried her best to act hopeful. *It can't do any harm*, she thought, *and it will make Mother and Father happy.*

"Would you like me to put on a play imagining a happy ending with the hermits?" she asked, a week after their return. Her parents were in the auditorium of the puppet theater. Before, they'd been so absent; now they were around every moment. It was awful watching them weep when they thought she wasn't looking.

Her father stirred. "A play? How delightful." The croak in his throat was almost gone.

Her mother attempted a smile. "Can we help you?"

Angela glowed. "Would you like to?"

In no time, the count was building the set; the countess was making hermit puppets with big pearl buttons for eyes and a shag of white yarn for beards; Nurse was knitting costumes; and Angela was putting quill to parchment, composing the noblest of speeches.

That night she performed the piece for her audience of three. It was a romantic comedy starring Peter, his fellow hermits, the Boy—cast as a lowly goatherd—and Angela Gabriela, Avenger of God. After many adventures and a few songs, the loyal comrades destroyed the evil forces of Archduke Arnulf and his henchmen.

Her parents laughed and applauded. Even Nurse had a good time.

Basking in their attention, Angela thrilled at a curious discovery. The more she acted happy and hopeful, the happier and more hopeful she became. By pretending hard enough, she'd made her make-believe feelings real.

At least in the moment. That night, her terrors returned. She dreamed she was being drowned in a tub of milk, strangled with ribbons, and tossed from a parapet.

So it continued: days of play and nights of terror. As the archduke's arrival drew near, the terror spilled more frequently into the light until all pretending of hope and happiness disappeared and she lived in dread from waking to waking.

The night before she was to be taken, Angela slid into a nightmare that felt as real as it was terrifying. She was chased through a dark forest by an unseen monster. Angela fell. She couldn't get up. The creature stood over her. It was the Necromancer. "I have what you need," he said, and disappeared.

Angela woke up, the dream's meaning as clear as rainwater. Everyone said the Necromancer had potions, and that's *exactly* what she needed. A potion like the one in the story her tutor had told her. It concerned two feuding families. A girl her age loved a boy from the enemy family, but was engaged to her older cousin. To avoid the marriage, she took a potion that made her appear dead.

Unfortunately, the story didn't turn out very well—in fact the girl and boy both died—but Angela was sure her ending would be much better. When the archduke arrived, she'd take the Necromancer's potion and fall to the floor in a deathlike sleep. Arnulf would see her buried in her family's crypt and go back to his palace. Her parents would untomb her and spirit her to Peter the Hermit, where she'd live in secret, happily ever after.

Angela jumped out of bed. She had to get to the Necromancer at once. Should she tell her mother and father? No. They might try to stop her. At the very least they'd insist on coming along for protection. She'd have liked that, but she had no intention of putting them in danger.

The clock in the corridor struck midnight. There was no time to waste. Angela tiptoed down the sleeping hallway to her father's study, where she borrowed a gold coin from the secret compartment in his desktop, and from there up to her turret theater, where she grabbed a beggar-woman costume and Nurse's endless woolen shawl. Then, armed only with hope, she slipped from the castle to search for the Necromancer in Potter's Field.

10

THE DANGEROUS MISSION

*A*ngela made her way down Castle Hill rehearsing the speech she'd prepared in case anyone gave her trouble. It was a line from one of her plays: "I have business with the Necromancer. You'd best leave me be, or he shall see you to the gates of Hell." She skulked as she imagined a creature of the night might skulk, keeping to the shadows as she passed by the mill and on through the village. Soon she was at the churchyard. Beyond lay Potter's Field.

Having never consulted the Necromancer, Angela wasn't sure how to find him. In her puppet plays, she'd imagined he'd have a little fire to guide the way, but there was none. Nurse had told her that villagers sought him out to contact the dead, or to cast spells to ruin their enemies' crops or turn their babies into cabbages. So she hid behind a bush, intending to follow one of them.

An hour later, she was still waiting. *I could be waiting forever*, she thought. *I'll have to go on my own.* Angela picked herself up, imagined the field was a giant stage, and made her entrance.

It was hard to see where to go. A blanket of cloud had blown in; the moon and the stars were tucked in bed. She swept the air in front of her to avoid running into bushes, but still stubbed her toes on brick grave markers. The biggest problem was Nurse's shawl. The coarse knit snagged on things unseen as if fingers were reaching out of the night to pinch her. And the wool rubbing against her ears sounded like creatures whispering.

Angela stood still. The sounds and the pulling stopped. "Who's there?"

Silence.

I'm imagining things. Angela shivered. She glanced back to where the village should have been, but every last candle had been extinguished. Where was she exactly? She removed the shawl from her head and spun in a circle. Everywhere was nowhere.

That's when she heard it. A slow, rhythmic tapping. No, not a tapping. What then? A thudding? A thunking? Whatever it was, it was something, somewhere—and something somewhere was better than nothing nowhere.

Angela hurried toward the sound. As she got closer, she heard murmurs and grunts, and saw a tiny light struggling against the night. She ran, catching her foot in the entrance to a weasel's den. She cried out.

The light disappeared. The thudding and grunts stopped too. Now what she heard was a curse and a scramble.

"Stop! Wait! I know you're there!" she shouted, and ran even faster toward where the light had been. The ground disappeared. She fell through the air and landed on something hard. It felt like rotting boards. Earth stretched up on either side of her. There was the most horrible stench she'd ever smelled.

She felt up the wall of earth. How would she ever escape? The wood under her feet gave way. Her ankles sank into something squishy. Frantic, she tried to claw her way out, but only loosened the dirt. It fell in her eyes and mouth. She feared the hole would cave in on her. "Help! Please! Come back!"

A hand reached down and gripped her own. "Who are you?" she gasped. "*What* are you?" There was no answer. Angela took this as her cue: "I have business with the

Necromancer. You'd best leave me be, or he shall see you to the gates of Hell."

"You've got business with the Necromancer?"

"Indeed I do," Angela said in her best heroic voice. "Take me to his dwelling that I might seek his power." The line had sounded much better in her theater. Still, it had the desired effect. Whoever it was hauled her out, opened the shutter on his lantern, and gasped.

"Little Countess!"

Angela was stunned. "Why, you're the Boy from the barrens!" She looked down into the hole. "I fell in a grave. Was the sound I heard you digging?"

Hans looked a little sheepish.

Angela gasped. "It was, wasn't it? You're a grave robber!"

"No, I'm not!"

This was true as far as it went. Hans had dug up the grave, but he'd yet to enter the Grand Society of Grave Robbers. All month, he'd slept outside the cave. He'd been soaked by thunderstorms, eaten by insects, and burned awake by the sun. Finally, he'd begged Knobbe to let him redeem himself. Tonight had been that chance. But the Little Countess had arrived and Knobbe had fled, leaving him in the worst of all worlds—a failure to his father and a villain to her.

"It's dangerous for you here," Hans said glumly. "Let me

guide you back to your castle."

"Not till I've seen the Necromancer."

From out of the night came a laugh as cold and dry as a rustle of birch leaves. "Ah, Little Countess, I've been expecting you."

11

IN THE NECROMANCER'S LAIR

The Necromancer floated into view, feeling his way with a long wooden staff. A wraithlike creature, hairless and pale, his willowy frame was draped in a dirty velvet shroud. His ears were withered; his nose and lips rotted. He had no teeth; no eyes. His sockets were empty caverns rippling with shadows from the lamplight.

"How long have you been there?" Angela whispered.

"Since the moment you thought of me," the Necromancer replied. With long, bony fingers, he withdrew two bird eggs from his dirty shroud and placed them in his eye sockets. "I've been watching you since you left your castle, my crow's eyes circling the night sky."

"Run!" Hans cried.

"Run yourself," Angela snapped.

"Yes, run yourself," the Necromancer purred.

"Little Countess, please, you don't know what he'll do, him and his gang of Weevils!" Hans pleaded. "It was them that told him you were here, you mark my word. Vicious boys—the kind that swarm the weak and torture cats. When I was a child, they tried to lure me into the dark. They—" His eyes went wide.

Angela looked over her shoulder. A dozen urchins lurked in the lantern light. A few held rocks in their hands; others sticks. They weren't more than ten years old, but there was a menace in their eyes that chilled Angela to the bone: These were the devils that had picked and poked at her in the dark.

The Necromancer's lizard tongue darted between gray gums. "The countess and I have business, boy. Go, lest I send my pets to your cave."

Hans stumbled backward and ran.

The Necromancer turned to Angela. "My lady."

The lantern went out. The world went dark. Angela heard low whistles from the Weevils. Why hadn't she fled when she'd had the chance?

"You didn't flee because you had no choice," the Necromancer said in her ear. "It was either me or marriage and death with the archduke."

Angela jumped. How had the Necromancer crept up behind her? How had he read her mind? It didn't matter. There was no turning back. She was trapped alone in the night with a living nightmare and a gang of savage boys.

"Necromancer, I seek . . . I seek . . ."

"I know."

"I can pay."

"I know."

Angela's flesh crawled as he sniffed the air around her. "Necromancer." She struggled to steady her voice. "If I return to the castle alive, I shall have more gold to give you."

"You think I want gold?"

"Don't you? I thought people from the village . . ."

"You're not from the village," the Necromancer said. He took her hand, and led her through the dark, guided by the smell and the taste of the night.

"Where are you taking me?" She tried to pull away, but the grip of his claws was fiercer than the archduke's iron fist.

They entered a thicket; the Necromancer released her. Angela tried to run but wherever she turned she was cut by thorns. She dropped to her knees in tears. Would she ever see her parents again?

Behind her, she heard a hollow grind; something was

opening. The Necromancer reached through the dark, lifted her to her feet, and led her down a staircase into the ground. The opening scraped shut.

The Necromancer snapped his fingers. A lamp flared overhead.

Angela was in an earthen room. Roots grew down from the ceiling. Worms crawled out of the walls. A dozen rickety cages were stacked along the back wall, each holding a pet crow. Along the sides of the room, rough shelves held countless bowls and jars of herbs, insects, and animal parts. Piles of bones lay in the corners. Under the lamp was a small table with the top half of an upturned skull. Three rotted teeth were embedded in the bone.

"Am I going to die?" Angela asked.

"Not yet," the Necromancer said.

Angela's eyes widened in alarm. "What do you mean, 'not *yet*.'"

"Come now, no need to be frightened. I mean simply that we all have a time and place appointed. You came to me for a potion. I've brought you here to receive it."

Angela collapsed in relief. "Thank you, Necromancer." Her hand shaking, she produced the gold coin she'd borrowed from her father's study. "For your troubles."

The Necromancer took the coin from her fingers as easily as if he had eyes. He read it with the tip of his tongue

62

and nibbled it with his gums. He twirled his fingers. It disappeared into thin air. "Sit against the wall."

Once Angela was settled, he rubbed a little spit into the skull. "Now then," he muttered, "a bit of this, a bit of that." His hands flew around the room depositing pinches of herbs, fungi, and insect parts into his bony mixing bowl. Then he cracked the crows' eggs in his sockets. The yolks slid down his cheeks and off his chin into the skull. He stirred furiously, cackling in ancient languages, while the crows cawed from their cages. At last he drained the lumpy mixture into a glass vial and held it to her nose.

"A taste of my work, and you shall appear dead for twelve hours," he said. "After that, you shall awake to your destiny."

Angela felt a chill. . . .

The next thing Angela knew, she was at the churchyard. The vial was in a cloth bag around her neck. Hans was beside her.

"Are you all right?" he asked.

"I don't know." Angela blinked. "How did I get here?"

"I dragged you back from where the Necromancer left you."

"How did you find me? You ran away."

"Not far, I didn't. I followed you by the sound of your

feet. You vanished into the thistle patch. A few minutes later, he brought you out and dumped you by the dead tree."

"It was brave of you to come after me," she said.

He looked at the ground. "I'm not brave."

There was a haze in the air. It would soon be dawn.

"Shall I walk you back to the castle?" Hans asked.

"Thank you, but I can manage by myself."

"Don't be so sure. The Weevils are still about."

Angela hesitated. "Well . . . if you've nothing else to do."

They walked in silence. Hans shot her shy glances; Angela pretended to be calm. He showed her the shortcut through the fields. When they reached the ditch at the foot of Castle Hill, they stopped and stared at each other, neither knowing what to say.

"I just realized," Angela blurted, "I don't even know your name."

"It's Hans."

"Hans?"

He blushed. "Yes, Hans. A name as simple and unimportant as myself."

She wanted to say, *But you're not unimportant. You're the mysterious boy from the barrens. The hero and villain in most of my plays.* Instead, all she said was, "I'm Angela."

He nodded.

"Well then, Hans . . . I guess I should say thank you . . . and . . . well . . . good-bye." Before she did something embarrassing, Angela hurried up the hill. She could feel Hans' eyes behind her, watching out for her from the ditch. A new and delicious sensation tingled across her forehead.

"Hans." She smiled to herself, the very sound of his name a delight. "Hans. Hans. Hans."

12

BURIED ALIVE

"In twelve hours I'll wake up and you'll rescue me from the crypt," Angela told her parents.

She was alone with them in their room, where she'd gone immediately on her return, thinking it wise to reveal her plan while they were still in bed. This way they'd be too groggy to be truly angry, and her mother wouldn't bang her head on the floor if she fainted. Most important, Angela could avoid the long ears of the servants, who loved nothing better than to gossip over their bowls of porridge. Nurse in particular had a tongue that could tease a tale into tomorrow.

She'd anticipated her parents' shock, though she'd

imagined a prettier speech from her father than: "Dear Lord, what did you do?!?"

Angela gave her a mother a whiff of the smelling salts she'd brought along for the occasion. "The Necromancer's potion is the only thing that stands between me and certain death," she pleaded.

Her parents had to admit it was true.

"There are roles you must play for the trickery to succeed," Angela said. "Father, to avoid suspicion, busy yourself about the estate as if preparing for a joyous occasion. Also, send for the priest to bless the archduke's arrival. If he's here, my burial can happen at once."

"Your burial," her mother repeated, blind with fear.

"Mother, please, I need you to be calm," Angela said firmly. Her mother gripped the bedsheets for comfort; the count placed a hand on her shoulder. "Your job, Mother, is to keep Nurse busy with the bridal baggage and to arrange bouquets for a banquet in the archduke's honor. The flowers should also make a nice effect at my funeral."

Her mother shivered. Angela held her gaze. "When the arrangements are complete, go to your sitting room and watch for the archduke. The moment you see his carriage, run up the stairs. You'll find me fallen. Hide the empty potion bottle in your bodice and raise the alarm." She held her parents' hands. "Let this be the performance of our lives."

Angela went to her theater to count down the final hours. The time between each tick and tock of the clock took forever. At last, just as she was tempted to leave the window to play with her puppets, she saw the telltale cloud of dust kicked up by the archduke's horses as they swept out of the village for the castle.

Her head swam. She gripped the ledge of the turret window. *Concentrate*, she told herself. She withdrew the potion from her pocket and lay down on the floor. After all, there was no point taking the potion standing. Who knew how her dress might end up? She struck the kind of death pose she'd seen in various great paintings.

Her mother burst into the room and ran to her side.

"Promise you'll be there when I wake up," Angela whispered. "Don't leave me with the dead."

"Never fear."

Angela gave her mother a smile. "I love you."

Her mother cradled her. "And I love *you*."

Angela raised the potion to her lips and drank.

Archduke Arnulf arrived to find a messenger racing to the village, and the castle in turmoil. Upstairs, he discovered the count and countess tearing at their wigs, the priest administering last rites, and his bride-to-be as cold and clammy as frogs in November.

"Dead?" Arnulf erupted. "How dare she be dead?"

"It was the sight of your carriage," the countess wept. "Our little angel dropped dead of delight."

Arnulf held a mirror to Angela's nose; no breath misted the glass. He blew into her eyes; not a hint of a blink. He listened for a heartbeat that never came. At last, he stood back and observed the artful positioning of the body. "At least she wasn't clumsy."

"Let us bury her now while there's luster in her cheeks," the count moaned. "There's a coffin in the family tomb that was made for me. May it house my darling."

"As you wish," Arnulf said. "I haven't time to waste on a dead girl. Yet give me the clothes she died in. I'd have them for my collection."

Within the hour, Angela was ready for burial in a plain white gown. She was placed on a gilt litter, scattered with violets and forget-me-nots, and carried by six footmen to the von Schwanenberg family crypt. It had been built centuries before in a small grove not far from the base of Castle Hill. Windowless and stern with stone walls a foot thick, the tomb gasped for air when its iron doors were thrown wide.

The town had emptied at word of Angela's death, villagers flooding to the estate to honor the Little Countess. Servants led them to the crypt, where they observed a prayerful silence, both out of respect for Angela and fear of the archduke, whose men lounged against some nearby trees.

Among the mourners was a young man with a pale complexion ruddied by clay. He'd visited many graves in his short life, but this was the first time he'd cried.

When the priest gave the final blessing, Angela's father carried her body into the tomb. Mahogany caskets, eight shelves high, circled the spacious vault, feet to the middle, like petals on a daisy. Angela's coffin was placed dead center.

The count and countess adjusted their daughter's curls on the lace pillow and placed her jewels and favorite things around her body: the locket with their portraits, the music box with the dancing ballerina, and the Angela Gabriela marionette. Then they sobbed into each other's arms.

Footmen moved forward to close the coffin. A dozen large carved rings ran along either side of the box and its lid. When the lid was lowered, the rings formed solid, parallel walls of interlocked teeth. Sturdy decorative poles, likewise of mahogany, slid through the ring holes and sealed the coffin shut.

"When you've finished with the tears," Arnulf said to the grieving parents, "pray accompany me to my carriage."

The count and countess did as they were told, expecting to receive private condolences. To their surprise, no sooner were they seated than the carriage began to move. It turned onto the public road. Angela's parents froze before Arnulf like mice before a snake, but when the carriage entered the village, the count could hold his tongue no longer.

"Where are we going?" he asked nervously.

"Home," Arnulf yawned, and peered out the window.

The countess pictured Angela waking in her coffin. "But we must remain here. We have urgent business to attend to."

"Such as?"

"Such as . . . mourning," the count stammered.

"You'll be able to mourn where you're going," the archduke said.

"Where is that?"

"The lunatic asylum."

"I don't understand," the countess gasped.

"Oh, but I think you do."

They'd reached the far end of Potter's Field. A skeletal creature in a dirty velvet shroud stood by the ditch, a flock of crows circling above his head. The carriage stopped. Arnulf opened the door.

"Necromancer!" the count and countess exclaimed.

"How delightful to be reacquainted with the parents of Angela Gabriela," the Necromancer said. He entered the carriage. Angela's gold coin glittered like a ghastly monocle in his left eye socket.

"The girl appeared quite dead, Necromancer," Arnulf said. "You brew a fine potion."

The Necromancer cast a sly smile. "The recipe's been in my family for centuries."

Arnulf leaned forward. "The Necromancer stopped my carriage on the way to your castle and alerted me to your treachery. In reward, I've made him my lord high chancellor, with orders to use his power to ferret out the archduchy's traitors."

The Necromancer grinned at the count and countess. "Imagine: I, whom you treated as a leper, have become the archduke's highest in command. The gods are just." He nodded to the archduke. "I shall miss my little root cellar. Yet I shall take consolation in your catacombs. Yea, and in sending my little gang of Weevils to every corner of the land."

The countess gripped her fan. "How did you know Angela wanted the potion to avoid her wedding?"

The Necromancer splayed his bony fingers across his withered chest. "How could I not? When a bride-to-be wishes to feign death, what else can one think? They say I have no heart. But I can read one."

The count swallowed hard. "Archduke, our Angela wakes at midnight. Please, spare her. Return to the castle at once."

"What for?" Arnulf asked. "If the walls were less thick, we might have enjoyed a picnic in the grove, serenaded by her melody of terror. As it is, the crypt will mute her screams to silence."

"But she'll be buried alive!"

"That's the general idea, yes."

The countess convulsed in wails as the count lunged for the archduke. Arnulf subdued him with the flick of an iron finger. "What fun to imagine your Angela waking in her coffin. She tries to stretch. Oh dear, a little cramped? She tries to breathe. Oh my, a little stuffy? But one thing she can surely do is scream. Scream and scream for her mother and father—who will never come."

13

THE DEAD AWAKEN

The sun went down. The hour grew late. The potion was wearing off. A faint pulse warmed Angela's flesh. Her pupils flickered beneath her eyelids. She was having a dream. A very bad dream.

She was a puppet in a play, and all of her scenes were being changed by Archduke Arnulf. "What are my lines? What do I say now?"

The other puppets stared at her. "Aren't you the girl who knows everything?"

She tried to run from the stage, but kept falling, her legs tangled up in her strings. The more she struggled, the more tangled she became. The lights went out. She was tossed into a storage box.

A voice came out of the dark. "Perhaps your puppet plays aren't so silly after all." It was Georgina von Hoffen-Toffen, smelling of stale milk and buzzing with flies.

Angela was puzzled. "You're dead."

"Oh yes, quite dead," Georgina agreed. "Soon you will be too. We shall be sisters."

That's when Angela realized she was having a nightmare.

"It's a pity you were murdered by the archduke," she told Georgina. "I truly wish I hadn't laughed. But all the same, if you don't mind, I'm going to wake up now."

Angela scrunched her nose and thought wake-up thoughts like she always did to get herself out of bad dreams. But when she blinked herself awake, she found herself in a place like her nightmare: a cramped, suffocating box without sound or light. Except this place was worse. This place was real.

Where could I be? she wondered. *Oh no! My plan. I'm sealed in a coffin. Locked in a vault with the dead.*

Angela banged frantically against the lid. It didn't budge.

She took a deep breath. Another. Another. All would be well. Her parents would arrive; they'd save her.

But time passed. They didn't arrive. More time passed. Still nothing. Cold sweat drenched her body. Something had gone wrong. Her parents weren't coming. Not now. Not ever.

The air was going bad. Soon it would be gone and she would drift into a sleep from which there would be no waking.

Angela clawed at the lid. "Help! Somebody, help! I can't die like this! No!"

Angela had always hated stories with bad endings. So, as she heard the ghostly voice of Georgina calling her to unconsciousness, she summoned her courage. "I planned a comedy," she announced to the darkness. "That means a happy ending. Do you hear me? A happy ending! I insist on it!"

14

THE INITIATION

Hans returned home from the funeral. All day and into the early night, he'd wandered aimlessly with his grief. Now all he wanted was to close his eyes and make the world go away. His father wouldn't let him.

"Tonight's your third and final chance to join the Grand Society of Grave Robbers," Knobbe said, lugging the tools of their trade from the cave.

"What?"

"You must rob the von Schwanenberg family crypt. That Little Countess will have treasure galore. Her parents spared nothing in their grief."

Hans slumped by the fire pit. "Please, Papa, no."

77

Knobbe whapped him with a burlap bag. "It's as easy a job as ever there was. I built a tunnel into the tomb years ago to relieve the count's ancestors of their pretties. The entrance is hidden with rocks and brambles, but a five-minute dig will clear it. Then it's a short crawl to a fortune."

"Can't we give the dead a night's peace?"

"Not on your life! The archduke's soldiers are plundering the castle as we speak. Come morning, they'll turn their thievery to the tomb. By the time they've picked it clean, there'll be nothing left for honest souls like us."

Hans buried his head in his hands. "I can't rob Angela's grave! I can't."

Knobbe scratched his butt. "Who are you to call the Little Countess by name?"

"It's none of your business."

"Are you in love with a dead girl?" Knobbe laughed.

Hans' cheeks burned. "She was my friend."

"Oh, to be sure," Knobbe mocked. "A fine friend. Her a countess and you a grave robber's apprentice."

Hans grabbed a rock and leaped to his feet. Knobbe jumped back. Hans stared at the rock in shock. He threw it away and burst into tears.

Knobbe peered in puzzlement at his son. He had no idea why the lad was crying, or why he felt his own heart melt. Was he having a spell? Or maybe gas? To his horror, Knobbe suddenly realized that what he was feeling was feelings. Well, feelings weren't going to rob him of a fortune.

He gave Hans' shoulder a squeeze. "I don't know about love," he muttered gruffly. "But your Angela's gone. Them tears won't bring her back, neither. Even so, you can save her precious burial things. If you don't, they'll be looted and dirtied, by the archduke's soldiers. Is that what you want?"

Hans shook his head. His father was right. Angela's keepsakes must be protected. He'd return them when the soldiers were gone. He wiped his eyes. "Let's go."

Angela was dimly aware of a distant thudding, thumping, whumping sound. "They're coming for me," she murmured from the land between life and death.

"They've come too late," Georgina replied, batting flies from her curdled ringlets.

Angela heard someone wriggling under the ground beneath the tomb. The sound of a heavy tile being pushed up and shoved along the floor. The sound of someone grunting into the crypt.

"They're coming for me . . . coming for . . ." Her voice drifted into another world, a world in which she cried silently, *Here! I'm in here.*

Hans emerged with his lantern in the far corner of the vault. He had to work quickly: Arnulf's soldiers could arrive at any moment. Hans squeezed between two rows of coffins and wriggled to the center of the room.

Angela's casket was in front of him, resting on a dais. Hans set down his lantern and wrestled the heavy poles through the row of interlocking rings on each side. A mighty push and the lid slid sideways, crashing to the floor.

Hans took the bag off his shoulder and filled it with Angela's treasures. He never looked at her face. If he did, he knew he'd run and fail her. But when his work was done, he leaned against the coffin and gazed down. "Forgive me. If I hadn't been a coward, I wouldn't have let the Necromancer chase me away. He's the reason you're dead, isn't he? *I'm* the reason you're dead."

Hans noticed something peculiar. Angela's hands were faced palms up on either side of her head. He took them to lay them properly.

Without warning, the corpse grabbed him, opened its eyes, and sat up.

Hans screamed.

Angela screamed, too. She let go of Hans, who fell to the floor, and gulped for air. "So you came for me at last! Thank heaven! Did my parents send you? What kept you so long?"

"I—I—I—you—you—you—" Hans scuttled backward.

"What's the matter?" Angela demanded.

"You're dead!"

For the first time, Angela noticed his terror. "If you thought I was dead, what are you doing here?" The answer was obvious. "My jewels!" she exclaimed, pointing at the trail of gems that led to the burlap sack at his side. "You came to rob my grave! Just wait till my parents find out!"

"It's not what you think!"

"Don't tell me what I think!" Angela roared, and stormed out of her coffin.

Hans ran between the burial shelves, hopped down into the tunnel and crawled away as fast as he could.

Angela scooped the jewels into the abandoned sack, grabbed the lantern, and followed in hot pursuit. But when she emerged into the moonlight, she saw him yattering wildly to a monk with a shovel. Angela didn't know what they were saying, but she was pretty sure she didn't want to stick around to find out.

"Alive?" Knobbe exploded. "What do you mean, the Little Countess is alive?"

Hans pointed at Angela, vanishing into the night. "*That's* what I mean."

Knobbe's knees knocked. "After her, boy! Take my shovel! Give her a whack on the head."

"What?"

"Put her back in that tomb!"

"You want me to kill Angela?"

"She's seen you, boy! She knows your name! It's her or us. Finish her off, or we swing at the end of a rope!"

"No!"

Knobbe's eyes bulged. "What do you mean, no?"

"I mean I can't. I won't. She's Angela."

"This is no time for feelings, boy."

"I don't care."

"How dare you defy me?" Knobbe railed. "After all the honors I've given you! You shame the Grand Society of Grave Robbers!"

"What Grand Society?" Hans shouted, the words bubbling faster than his thoughts. "Who else belongs? Where do you meet?" He saw the flicker in his father's eyes. "There is no Grand Society, is there? It's only you. It's only ever been you."

"You calling me a liar?" Knobbe threatened.

"It's what you are," Hans cried, hurt and anger pounding in his head. "The Grand Society of Grave Robbers. Ha! You made it up to seem important. So I'd grow up to be your slave."

Knobbe howled and punched the handle of his shovel into Hans' stomach. Hans dropped to the ground. "It's your fault the girl must die," Knobbe said. "You're the one what let her see you. Her parents are taken. Her servants have fled. The job will be easy. Do it, now, or I will!"

15

THE HAUNTED CASTLE

ngela sprinted up the hill to the castle. Where were her parents? Why hadn't they come? She paused at the gate. Maybe the archduke was still inside. Maybe that's why they were delayed. Her eyes searched for his carriage. It was gone. So were the sentries. The castle doors were wide open.

Something was wrong. Angela blew out Hans' lantern, set it down, and crept inside. The place was ransacked. Draperies were ripped from the windows, furniture broken, tapestries stripped from the walls. What had happened to her parents? She raced up the main staircase to find them.

"Halt! Who goes there?" Six drunken soldiers staggered

into the hall from a side room. One held a silver candelabrum. They stood at the foot of the stairs and squinted up into the shadows.

"Why, if it isn't a serving wench," snickered one with a pig nose.

What will they do to me? Angela panicked. Her eyes fell on a pool of moonlight that shone through the entrance windows and spilled across the steps below her.

Angela had an inspiration. She rolled her eyes up into her head, let out a tickle of otherworldly laughter, and slowly descended the staircase. As she floated into the light, the soldiers' eyes bugged wide. Her hair was wild and matted; her face dripped sweat; her frock was sullied by mud. In the pale moon, the stains on her clothes resembled mold, and her sweat a glistening ooze of decay.

"That's no serving wench!" a soldier gulped. "It's the dead girl! The Little Countess!"

"We saw you buried!" screamed a second.

"Her ghost's returned!" hollered a third.

The soldiers scrambled over each other to escape. "Haunted!" they shrieked as they raced to their horses and galloped into the night. "The castle's haunted!"

Angela flew to her parents' rooms. They'd been plundered. She dashed to her theater. It, too, was destroyed: the stage smashed, the puppets stolen, the pillow people dismembered. She heard a sound from under the stage curtain crumpled in the corner: a great wheezing snore like a hog at market.

"Nurse!"

Nurse lurched awake. At the sight of her Little Countess, she babbled and crossed herself. It took five minutes for Angela to convince her she wasn't dead, and another five to explain what had happened. "But where are my parents?"

Nurse wrung her hands. "On the road to the capital. They've been arrested."

"Mother! Father!" Angela cried out, her mind alive with the wails she'd heard rising from the palace grates. "The Necromancer betrayed us. He was the only one who knew about the potion. And what of the servants?"

"All fled, save me. I hid under this curtain."

"Poor Nurse!"

"Poor Nurse, nothing," said she. "Had those ruffians assailed my virtue, I'd have had at them with my knitting needles!" The vigor of her voice surprised her. She crouched in fright. "They've all gone?"

"Yes," Angela nodded. "But when they tell the archduke they saw a ghost, he'll know I escaped and return to kill me."

"May they never reach him," Nurse quivered.

"No, God speed them. News I survived will give my parents hope."

"Let's keep that hope alive," Nurse said. "We'll hide you in the village."

Angela shook her head. "The village is the first place Arnulf will look. I must flee to the country to plan the rescue of my parents."

"The rescue of your parents? It's impossible."

"Nothing is impossible." Angela ran to the pile of pillow-people stuffing and rummaged about for General Confusion's coat, boots, breeches, and helmet.

"This isn't one of your plays," Nurse pleaded. "What are you thinking? A rescue? And launched from the country? What do you know of the country?"

Angela pretended not to hear: If Nurse was flustered by the country, she'd have a heart attack knowing she planned to race all the way to Peter the Hermit's. Angela swam into the general's outfit, rolled up the sleeves and breeches, and stuffed the toes of the boots with Mistress Tosspot's handkerchiefs. The helmet was large enough to conceal her hair, and the coat sufficiently roomy to hide her sack of burial jewels.

Angela saw Nurse squeezing herself into Lord Forgetful's velvet pantaloons. "What are you doing?"

"Donning my own disguise," Nurse grunted. "You hardly think I'd let my Little Countess wander about by herself, do you? What, while her mind's beset by wild ideas?"

Angela gasped: Nurse could no more outrun danger

than she could fly. She waited till the good woman's head was lost in Lord Forgetful's undershirt, then ran from the turret. "Farewell, Nurse," she called over her shoulder. "I promise you'll see me and my parents alive and home again."

THE ROAD TO ADVENTURE

Angela bolted down Castle Hill. Ahead the open road beckoned to the great forest and the snow-capped mountains beyond. In no time she'd be plotting the rescue of her parents with Peter the Hermit. Angela had no idea how she and a raggedy hermit could penetrate the palace, but stranger things had happened, at least in books.

Lost in the future, Angela was unprepared for the present. A hooded monk leaped from the ditch wielding a shovel. Angela fell backward, her helmet toppling from her head. The monk stood over her.

"You're the old man with Hans, aren't you?" she said,

scrambling to retrieve the sack from beneath her general's coat. "Here are the burial jewels you wanted. Just spare me."

"I don't want your jewels. I knew the archduke's men would steal them. I wanted to keep them safe."

Angela recognized the voice. "Hans?"

"Yes." Hans threw back the hood. "You were right to fear me. I was told to kill you. I refused."

Angela glanced fearfully at the bushes. "Where's the old man?"

His voice wavered: "I knocked him out." He sucked in a breath.

"What's the matter?"

"He was my papa. After tonight, he won't want to see me. Not ever." He wiped his eyes. "At least with you I won't be alone. Nor you with me. Wherever we go, we can help each other."

Angela shifted uncomfortably. "I'm sorry, Hans, I don't want your help."

"What?"

"I have to flee to a secret place. There'll be all sorts of perils: Highwaymen. Wolf packs. And if I survive, even worse. I'll be on a quest to free my parents from the devil himself: Archduke Arnulf and his necromancer! I need someone I can count on."

"That's me."

Angela sighed. "I like you, Hans, but at Potter's Field

and my family's crypt you ran away."

"You're saying I'm a coward?"

"Well," Angela said carefully. "You're not exactly brave. Anyway, sorry, I have to go." She grabbed her helmet and took off.

"Wait." Hans chased after her. "Take me with you, and I swear on my life, I'll never run away again."

"With a promise like that, you'll be dead by daybreak."

"All right, take me with you and I'll be your faithful knight."

"I wouldn't count on that either."

"What do you want then?" Hans implored.

"I'm not sure," Angela said, "but I'll know when I hear it."

Hans ran ahead and threw himself at her feet. "Angela, take me with you, and I'll do your bidding forever and ever."

"That's more like it," Angela said brightly. "I could use a servant."

"A servant?" Hans leaped up. "You want me to be your servant?"

"Why, yes," Angela beamed. "I've never been without one."

"I'm nobody's servant."

"Well, you are now. Unless you're a liar. After all, you *did* say you'd do my bidding forever and ever."

"You tricked me!"

"I most certainly did not. So which are you? A liar or a servant? Make up your mind. I have to go."

"Oh!" Hans jumped in the air in frustration. "Fine then! I'm your servant!"

"I'm so glad!" Angela exclaimed. With that, she adjusted her general's coat and marched up the road, the grave robber's apprentice at her heels.

ACT II

The Wolf King

17
UNPLEASANT NEWS

*I*t was three in the morning. Arnulf was camped at a royal stables two hours from County Schwanenberg. His troops had enjoyed a feast of wild boar and wine, while he and the Necromancer tormented the count and countess. The soldiers were now passed out in piles, but Arnulf and his new lord high chancellor continued to amuse themselves outside the carriage-prison.

"Mama, Papa, where are you?" Arnulf squeaked with a high-pitched wail. "Why have you left me to die?"

The count and countess sobbed into each other's arms.

The Necromancer laughed. His crows joined in with a chorus of caws from their perch on the carriage roof.

Arnulf leered through the window bars. "Tell me, Lord High Chancellor, do you suppose the girl is still living? Is she sucking her final breaths?"

The Necromancer cocked an ear stump as if transporting himself inside the tomb. "Why, yes, Excellency, she lives," he rasped. "But I fear the poor thing's fingers are bloodied from clawing at the coffin lid."

"Kill us now," the countess wept. "Spare us this torture."

"And spoil the entertainment?" Arnulf tutted.

A cry broke the night air: "Haunted! The castle's haunted!" Arnulf's soldiers roused as their six terrified comrades galloped into the encampment and collapsed on the ground. "The Little Countess," gasped one. "She's come back from the grave."

"What?"

"We saw her in the castle. Gliding down the staircase. Glistening in the moonlight."

"It's true," said another. "All of us—we saw her ghost!"

"That was no ghost," Arnulf shouted. "That was the Little Countess in the flesh."

"Your Highness, we were at her funeral. We saw her dead and buried."

"She wasn't dead, you idiot. She was buried *alive!*"

Cries of rapture erupted from Angela's parents. "Our child outfoxed you," the count taunted.

Arnulf strode to the carriage and gripped the bars so

hard they bent. "Your joy shall be as short-lived as your daughter's life," he hissed, and swung back to his troops. "Because of you, I've been tricked by a child and mocked by my own captives! Find her or die."

"Wh-where would you have us search?" stammered the bravest.

The Necromancer swept his staff through the air: "Excellency, there's a local grave robber who lives with his apprentice on the barrens. It's likely they broke into the crypt, allowing the girl's escape."

"Come with us," Arnulf ordered his bodyguards. "We'll find this grave robber and make him talk. As for the rest of you, tie the traitors in sacks, toss them on a wagon, and bounce them to the booby hatch."

18

THE ROAD NORTH

Hans and Angela trekked north by moonlight. The journey was slow. Under the stars, even familiar sights turned into dreamscapes.

"I wish we had a lantern," Angela said.

"Not me," Hans replied. "The archduke's soldiers will be questioning farmers for miles around. We don't want anyone to report us."

Angela stopped to remove a stone from her left boot. "I'm tired."

"How? You slept all day."

"I was drugged in a coffin."

"That's easier than worming along an old tunnel into a

crypt. Raising that stone slab off the floor nearly broke my shoulder."

"Grave robbing is your job," Angela sniffed. "You should be used to it. Besides, you don't have to walk in boots the size of wine barrels."

"No," Hans said. "I don't get any boots at all. I get bare feet, is what I get."

They trudged in silence.

"So . . . ," Hans said at last, "what's your plan?"

"What do you mean?"

"Well, where are we going, for one thing?"

"The hermitage in the far mountains," Angela said brightly.

Hans was stunned. "That's days away and another day climbing. What do you plan for us to eat till we get there? Where do you plan for us to sleep?"

Angela hadn't thought of those things. In her plays, journeys were accomplished in a scene change. In life, they were managed by servants. Still, she didn't want Hans to think she was an idiot. "I trust in Providence."

"The kind of Providence that got you buried alive?"

"Unburied, too, don't forget."

"I'd call that luck."

"That's because you don't know any better. Read whatever story you like: Something always turns up around the corner."

Angela was immediately proven right. Over the hill and around the next bend, torches illuminated a castle she recognized at once: Castle von Hoffen-Toffen, ancestral home of the wretched Georgina. As it had been the nearest titled household, her family had made seasonal visits. What a chore and a snore and a bore. Yet tonight Angela thrilled at the thought of its feather beds. She darted up the drive to the gates.

"What are you doing?" Hans cried in alarm.

"Count von Hoffen-Toffen is a friend of my parents," Angela called over her shoulder. "He's sure to help us. At the least to give us horses, maps, and a packet of dried mutton."

Hans raced to catch up. "Are you out of your mind? Friends of your family are sure to be questioned by the archduke."

"Count von Hoffen-Toffen would never betray me."

Hans grabbed her by the arm. "Says who?"

Angela shook him off. "I've no idea how you common folk conduct yourselves, but we nobles understand chivalry."

A flurry of hooves clattered down the castle drive. A pair of armed sentries confronted them, one with a torch and the other with a musket. "Who goes there?"

Angela lowered her chin; the rim of her helmet masked her face in shadow. "We have business with your master," she said in the voice of an old general. "You would do well to take us to him or he shall have you in irons."

The sentries eyed Hans and Angela warily.

"Who has business in the middle of the night?" said the sentry with the musket.

Angela fumbled in her bag of burial jewels and held up the gold locket with the miniatures of her parents. "Show him this. One look at the portraits and he'll know us as friends."

The sentry with the torch grabbed her by the arm. "How does a general get such delicate hands?"

The other sentry cocked his musket. "Look into the light, the pair of you."

Slowly, Angela raised her head, but the Little Countess familiar to the von Hoffen-Toffen court was unrecognizable in the grubby lass with matted hair.

"What kind of girl is loose at this hour?" demanded the sentry with the torch. "And what's a boy doing dressed as a monk?"

Hans and Angela said nothing.

The sentries marched them to the castle, where they sat on a stone bench under guard. The chief steward was duly summoned. He examined the jewelry bag and took it to Count von Hoffen-Toffen.

In short order, the count strode through the main arch-way in a burgundy dressing gown, lambskin slippers, and a nightcap with a tassel that waggled as freely as his chin. One glance at the creatures who'd woken him from his dream of frolicking milkmaids, and he was in high dudgeon. "I've never laid eyes on these ragamuffins."

Angela leaped to her feet. "Count von Hoffen-Toffen, you know me well. I'm the girl with the puppet theater in a turret of her family's castle. And I know one of your secrets: Georgina found mice nesting in your Easter wig."

The count rubbed his eyes. "Good heavens." He turned to Hans and covered his nose with his sleeve. "Who might you be?"

"A servant and a friend."

The count waved at his people. "Leave us." Once alone, he returned Angela's bag of jewels. "News arrived that you were dead, Countess, and your parents arrested for treason."

"Only half true, and that half barely," Angela said. "My parents were seized for trying to stop my marriage to the archduke. I'm running for my life to a friend who can help me save them."

"If your life is in peril, so are the lives of all who help you. You must leave my castle at once."

"What if Georgina had run to my father?" Angela implored him. "Should he have barred the door?"

The count looked away. "Georgina . . ."

"Count von Hoffen-Toffen," Hans said boldly. The count turned to him. Hans wanted to run, but held his ground. He took a deep breath and attempted to speak as nobly as Angela. "Though you could not save your daughter, you can save another. The countess and I have need of food, drink, and two of your horses. I pray you, mercy."

Von Hoffen-Toffen blinked at the boy's bearing. "My horses would be recognized," he said nervously, "but the kitchen can give you food. I dare not do more."

Supplied with a parcel of bread and cheese, Hans and Angela returned to the road. Angela looked at Hans in wonder. "Where did you learn to talk like an aristocrat?"

"Listening to you, I guess," Hans said sheepishly. "I sounded so stupid."

"Not at all, for a peasant. Court talk is a whole other language. You simply need to practice. It's lots of fun for playacting and for making good impressions. Grown-ups like it."

"None of the grown-ups I've ever known."

"Yes, well," Angela said. She decided to leave it at that.

The night was turning a deep blue.

"It'll be dawn soon," Hans said. "We better hide."

"Where?"

"There's an abandoned cemetery nearby where Papa used to dig," Hans said. "I'll poke around for an empty coffin tunnel."

19
THE BOUNTY BOX

When Knobbe came to at Angela's crypt, he was terrified: The punishment for stealing the property of a corpse was death; surely the punishment for stealing the property of a countess must be four deaths, maybe ten. Knobbe raced home and retrieved his bounty box, then hid in a rocky nook near the top of the cliff path by his cave.

Now it was nearly dawn. The grave robber ached in places he never knew existed. His body was pinched from the tiny hidey-hole, his joints throbbed from the damp cold of the rock, and his bowels were looser than the time he ate the dead bat from the village bell tower. Worst of all was the throbbing bump on the back of his head.

Had his boy really whacked him with a shovel, stolen his gear, and left him in his underrags? It was too cruel. Knobbe cradled his bounty box. "It's you and me," he said tenderly. "You's all I got left."

He looked to the sea. There was enough light to follow the roll of the waves and the murder of crows circling above. He decided to poke his head over the cliff top and look for intruders prowling the barrens.

Knobbe placed the wooden chest at the back of the nook and gave it a pat. "Never fear, my darling, I shall return." He hobbled onto the path and climbed up till he was level with the weeds at the summit. He peered between them. Peering back was a dirty twig of a thing, hair dancing with lice.

"What do you want, Weevil?"

The Weevil pointed over his shoulder to the grave robber's cave. Arnulf, the Necromancer, and a dozen soldiers were inspecting the entrance.

"I'm not here. You haven't seen me," Knobbe whispered.

The Weevil grinned, leaped to his feet, and waved both arms. "Over here."

"Shut up," Knobbe hissed.

"Over here," the Weevil hollered again. "I's found him. I's found him."

Knobbe spun around to escape down the cliff. Eight Weevils blocked his way, each with a reed spear. In his youth, Knobbe could've swung an arm and sent the pack flying. Now such a lurch would tumble him to his death.

"We see'd you at the crypt," the biggest Weevil snarled. "We followed you in the dark."

"Out of my way."

"Or what, old man?" The Weevil jabbed him with his spear.

Knobbe took a step back. "Please. Let me pass."

"Not so brave now, is you, old man? Not so fierce without your apprentice." The Weevil jabbed him again.

Knobbe fell to the path. The gang laughed. He clawed his way backward. "What have I ever done to you?"

"It's not what you's done. It's what you'll fetch us," snapped a Weevil with broken teeth. "Our master'll bless us. He'll feed us treats."

The Weevils swarmed, poking and prodding the grave robber to the summit. There they pinned him, while the Necromancer, Arnulf, and the soldiers gathered round.

"Well done, my pets," the Necromancer purred. He withdrew a dirty wad of toffee from his shroud and popped the goo into their mouths.

"You are Knobbe the Bent, grave robber of County Schwanenberg?" Arnulf demanded.

"I never robbed a grave in my life," Knobbe protested. "You want that boy of mine—he robbed every grave he could find."

"Come now," the Necromancer said, "we've long been neighbors. I know your hobby."

"I'm but a victim of lies," Knobbe cried. "Search my cave. You'll find no shovel nor bounty box."

Arnulf pressed his foot on Knobbe's throat. "Where is the Little Countess?"

"Dead in her crypt," Knobbe gurgled. "Ask the town. She died and was buried, poor thing."

"Excellency," the Necromancer intervened, "perhaps I can tickle his memory."

Arnulf stepped back. The Necromancer let forth a series of short, sharp caws. The circling crows landed around Knobbe's head. The Necromancer knelt beside him. "Listen well, old friend: My birdies prefer dead meat, but who can resist a fresh pair of eyeballs?"

"Please, no," Knobbe begged.

"Then tell us the truth: Where is the Little Countess?"

"I don't know. Truly."

A crow nipped his forehead.

Knobbe screamed. "The boy broke into her crypt. She was alive and ran for it. I told him to whack her, but he did me instead."

"Where are they?"

"Run off together, I expect."

The Necromancer faced Arnulf and swept his arm to the south. "That way lies the sea and drowning. To the east, bogs and quicksand. To the west, the road we took here. Therefore, our prey must be hidden in the village or fleeing north."

"How shall we catch them?"

"While you take your ease at Castle Schwanenberg, have your soldiers deposit my Weevils in town and along the road," the Necromancer said. "They'll hide under washtubs, and in coal bins, sludge pits, and stairwells. By dusk, they'll know every spot our little friends have stopped for refuge. Then I'll scoop them up and gut them for my spell pot."

Arnulf wiggled his iron digits. "Save me their pelts. I'll have hers for a pillowcase and his for a footstool."

Two Weevils yelped up the cliff path with Knobbe's bounty box. "Look what we's found!"

Arnulf went bone-white. He grabbed the chest in horror and stared at the inlaid teak. "Impossible." He dropped to the ground and threw open the lid. There before him was a carved crest of an eagle's head with lightning bolts, unicorns, and the sun. Arnulf trembled. "Her country's crest! It's hers indeed." He grabbed hold of Knobbe. "Where did this come from?"

"The sea," Knobbe quaked. "It swept in from the sea."

"When?"

"Twelve, thirteen years ago."

"What was in it?" Arnulf demanded.

"A baby. A little baby."

"Describe it."

"How?" Knobbe babbled. "It were a baby. It cried. It stank."

Arnulf shook him hard. "What marks upon its body?"

"None," Knobbe squealed, "save a spot upon its shoulder."

"What spot? Which shoulder?"

"The right," Knobbe blurted. "A birthmark shaped like an eagle."

Arnulf dropped the grave robber. He rose to his feet and staggered in circles. "They told me the child was dead," he raved. "They told me they killed him with his father." He whirled back to Knobbe. "What became of the boy?"

"Why, he's the lad I raised," Knobbe said. "The wretch who freed the Little Countess from the crypt."

"*Aaa!*" Arnulf shrieked to the heavens. "A thousand ducats for the skin of the grave robber's apprentice! And two thousand ducats for his head!"

20

THE HUNT

*H*ans and Angela entered the abandoned cemetery.
"Keep low," Hans said. "It's almost dawn."
He led her to an embankment far from the road. "People
hereabouts used to put concrete on top of their coffins to
ward off grave robbers, so Papa dug *across* from behind
slopes like this. He pulled off the end of the box, and took
what he wanted. Then he covered his tracks by plugging the
entrance with dirt and sod."

"How will you know where to look?"

"It's not the sort of thing you forget." Hans stopped. He
pressed his foot against a clump of dried weeds covering a
small hole. "This is the spot. It seems some animal's been

here before us." He scooped away the remains of the plug and peered up the tunnel. Two ribs and a kneecap littered the passage. "I need to do some housecleaning. Close your eyes."

Hans took a deep breath, imagined spring meadows, and entered the hole. In a few minutes, he crawled out. "After you, milady."

Angela knelt by the entranceway. "It stinks!"

"True enough," Hans said. "But after a day in a tomb and a night on the road, you don't smell so good yourself."

The day passed slowly.

In the village, gossip flowed as freely as the river by the mill; no one took heed of the grubby boys who loitered in the square and outside the shops. But on the road north, farmers paused in their fields and barns, as did their wives at wash pumps and chicken coops. There was a feeling of eyes and ears behind the sheaves, the sheds, the tubs, and the raspberry bushes: a feeling of something that watched what they did, and heard what they said.

Before the sun began to set, their animals were in their pens, their laundry was off the lines, and they were safe indoors with the shutters barred. Tonight would be a night of prayer; something evil was in the air.

At Castle von Hoffen-Toffen, the night watchmen took their positions as darkness filled the surrounding valleys, stretched across the count's fields, and swept up the drive to the castle gate.

There was a furtive scurry from behind a bank of rose-bushes. One of the sentries raised his torch. The other gripped his musket. "Who's there?"

A tall, thin stranger stepped out of the shadows. His empty eye sockets were packed with gold teeth.

"I would speak with the count," the stranger said, holding up a parchment with the royal seal. "I'm told you've had visitors."

Up the road, Hans and Angela scrambled out of their coffin tunnel. They'd spent a sleepless day. Whenever Angela's eyes had drifted shut, she'd imagined skeletons stroking her hair. Hans, too, had spent the day alert, gripping his wooden shovel.

Hans put weeds over the entrance to their hiding place. "We mustn't leave clues we've been here. And we need to avoid the village ahead. Too many eyes in taverns." He motioned to the fields behind them. "If we stick to where the farmhands have walked, our tracks will be lost in theirs."

"That's clever," Angela said.

"I know about escapes," Hans nodded proudly. "Three final dodges: We'll walk backward to the fields, so our foot-prints will look like they're coming *into* the cemetery. I'll step in your tracks so we'll look like we're only one person.

And we'll keep our hems high so they don't bend the grass."

By the time the pair had skirted the village and returned to the main road, twilight had given way to night. A wolf howled in the distance. Another answered its call.

"The great forest must be near," Hans said. "We can take cover in its trees."

"And expose ourselves to those beasts?"

"Better to beasts with four legs than with two," Hans replied. "Besides, wolves stay to themselves, except in stories."

"It's more than the wolves. I don't want to get lost."

"We can't if we keep to the tree line by the road," Hans said. "Trust me."

The Necromancer also heard the wolves as he and his Weevils left Castle von Hoffen-Toffen. He pictured them, too—he who'd been born without eyes—for he saw with his ears, his nose, his tongue, and his mind. What visions they'd brought him tonight.

The count had been brave, but the Necromancer had seen the terror beneath the calm: heard the rustle of the man's gown as his knees shook, and tasted the fear in the air from his short, quick breaths. Nor did he need eyes to see when the Weevils set the count's clothes alight. The smell of burning velvet had painted a picture; so did the splash when the count leaped down the well to douse the flames. It was so dramatic, the Necromancer had burst into applause.

There'd been other sensations as well: first, the sound of the servants' tongues as they'd flapped about the castle's visitors, and now the caws of his crows, as he entered the boneyard. His skin was prickling; the prey was near. For where but in a cemetery—his second home—would a grave robber's apprentice hide? And where in a cemetery but in a coffin tunnel?

The Necromancer prowled the back of the graveyard while his Weevils searched for tracks and his crows pecked for toads and other dainties. Soon, he'd found the slope and the entrance, the cover of weeds surrendering to his staff. He inhaled the tunnel's odor, caught the scent of the Little Countess. He flicked his tongue. They hadn't gone far. He could taste them in the air.

The Weevils ran up. "Master, they's vanished. No footprints leaves the cemetery. The only ones what enter comes from a single pair of boots arriving from the fields."

The Necromancer knew the tricks by heart. He lolled his head. "I see our prey walking backward in each other's steps," he droned. "I see them racing through the farm fields to the road north of the village."

The Weevils gasped.

The Necromancer chuckled. While he awed the mortal world with his second sight, his secret was plain.

Imagination and common sense: What else did one need to see both past and future?

"Our friends will be nearing the great forest," the Necromancer said. "They'll seek cover in its trees. Look to the muddy ditches. You'll see footprints where the pair has crossed over. Follow the trail of broken twigs and upturned leaves. Move quickly, my pets. Before dawn, they shall be ours."

21

THE GREAT FOREST

As Hans and Angela neared the great forest, Hans sang a tavern song about its most famous legend:

"The Wolf King has a monster horde
That fears nae mortals nae the Lord.
It eats fair damsels, slays their knights;
Such horrors be its true delights."

Like everyone else, Angela knew tales of the Wolf King. She'd even done a play about him and his monsters, hanging six ghastly creations from a rod and dragging them toward the Boy, whom she rescued with her Sword of Justice. Angela had been proud of the backdrops she'd painted of the great forest, but they didn't come close to matching the real thing. From the top of the turret on Castle Hill, she'd seen specks of green stretching along the horizon. What she saw now was a world of trees that towered on either side of the road as far as forever. No wonder there were tavern songs.

"The Wolf King's hunger is worst at night,
His fangs dismember all in sight—"

"Oh, be quiet," Angela said. "It's easy enough to imagine this place a home to trolls and witches."

"So you believe in fairy tales?" Hans grinned.

"Don't you? Can you imagine a witch worse than the Necromancer? And speaking of trolls, I've met your father. We need to be careful, Hans. This is a perfect place for evil to hide."

"Are you the same girl who ventured into Potter's Field alone?"

"Yes, and I learned my lesson."

"Oh?" Hans laughed. "You left alone for the far mountains right after I rescued you from the crypt."

"I had no choice," Angela exclaimed. "And, by the way, you didn't rescue me. You tried to rob me. I got out of the tomb by myself."

"What?" Hans exclaimed. "You're the most ungrateful person I've met!"

"Me? You're the one who should be grateful. If I hadn't let you come along as my servant, you'd be in your cave taking orders from a grave robber."

"Better that than taking orders from a spoiled brat who thinks she's better than everyone."

Angela wanted to say something smart, but what? He was right. A breeze whistled down the road between the banks of trees. She dug her hands into her coat and scrunched her shoulders till the stiff military collar covered her ears.

Hans held up his arm. "Sh." He cocked his ear. Angela heard something too. The breeze fell. Hans exhaled. "It's only the rustling of the leaves. Time to head for the trees before it's something real." He stepped into the ditch and walked backward. "Come on. What are you waiting for?"

"Nothing. It's just . . ." Angela's voice trailed off.

"You really *are* afraid, aren't you?" Hans laughed.

"No, I'm not," Angela lied. She stepped boldly backward into the ditch, slipped on the mud, and fell on her behind. Hans reached out to help her. "Leave me alone," she sputtered, and scrambled to her feet. "I don't need your help. I don't need anyone's help." She ran to the nearest tree and pressed her face into her arm.

Hans waited till her shoulders stopped heaving. "It's all right," he said gently. "Everyone gets scared."

"Not me," Angela said. "I'm a countess. It's not allowed."

"Well, I'm a boy. It's not allowed for me either."

Angela smiled despite herself. "Maybe we have something in common after all." She paused. "Hans, when I ran from the castle, courage was easy: I didn't have time to think. But now that I do, I *am* scared. Scared we won't get away. Scared what Arnulf will do if he gets us."

"It's brave of a countess to tell that to her servant," Hans said.

"You're more than my servant," she said shyly. "You know that, don't you?"

"I was hoping." He shuffled awkwardly. "I'm sorry I called you a spoiled brat."

"Why? It's the truth. If I'm not allowed to be scared, I mustn't be scared of the truth, either." Angela swallowed hard. "I've always had things given to me. I've never had to be nice. From now on, I promise to try and be better."

"I promise, too," Hans said. "I don't have shining armor, but I'll really do my best to be your knight."

"With a little acting, you could fit the part," Angela said. "It's how I imagined you in my plays. In some of them, anyway."

Hans didn't know whether to laugh or blush. So he did both. "Yes. Well." He adopted a courtly pose. "Shall we proceed, milady?"

Angela grinned. "Indeed, Sir Knight. Let's sally forth!"

• • •

Sallying forth was easier said than done. Within ten minutes, Hans had gotten tangled in a vine and Angela had tripped on a rotten stump. "If the Necromancer doesn't get us, the forest will," Angela muttered. "We're making enough noise to wake the dead. Meanwhile our enemies are on the move with torches."

"Then we'll see them coming." Hans stopped suddenly and pointed through the trees at something large on the road ahead. "Stay here." Angela didn't need convincing.

Hans crept along the side of the ditch as quiet as a moth on an overcoat. *I'm a knight, I'm a knight, I'm a knight*, he told himself.

The something was a horse and cart. A canvas cloth was draped over the wagon's contents. The owner was nowhere to be seen.

The owner must be sleeping in back with his belongings, Hans thought. *If he lived around here, he'd have brought the cart home. So he must be a traveler; someone with food and drink.* Hans paused. *What if he works for the archduke?*

A twig snapped behind him. Hans imagined the Weevil gang hanging from the branches. He looked over his shoulder. There was nothing but trees and dark.

Hans slipped across the ditch and crouched at the side of the road. The horse snorted and went back to sleep. Hans tiptoed to the back of the wagon and peeked under the covering. There were baskets of fruit and vegetables, and boxes and bundles of sundries.

He was about to fill the pockets of his robe when he felt a knife at his throat. The man with the knife leaned in. "Say your prayers."

22

THINGS THAT GO BUMP IN THE NIGHT

"I'm a simple monk in need," Hans pleaded.

"Don't camp on the road through the forest, they say, or the Wolf King will get ye," the man snarled in Hans' ear. "So I made me a bed in the roots of a tree, and sure if I don't wake to the sound of you sneaking up to my wagon. Well, you be no Wolf King nor monk, neither. A common thief is what you be, and you'll never again filch from me nor any other poor peddler." He readied his blade.

"Peddler!" a voice commanded from the trees. "Drop your weapon!"

The peddler squinted into the dark. An old general emerged from the forest, starlight glinting off his epaulettes and helmet. A musket was crooked at his shoulder, aimed at the peddler's head. The peddler fell to his knees and threw away his knife.

"For shame, threatening the life of a friar," Hans said.

"You speak to me of shame?" the peddler replied. "You a rogue monk and a rogue soldier?"

Angela came out of the shadows. "You wrong us, sir. We're not what we seem, nor what you imagine."

The peddler saw that "the general" was a girl holding a broken branch. "Who are you? What do you want?"

Hans had an inspiration. "We are humble travelers journeying to the far mountains," he said in his finest court talk. "What say you, friend: Is your wagon for hire?"

Angela had been wondering the same thing. A wagon was faster than foot, and the faster they got to the far mountains, the sooner they'd be safe from Arnulf and able to plot the rescue of her parents. She produced a diamond from her jewel sack. "Here's treasure for your pains."

The peddler bit the jewel and turned it in his fingers. "'Tis real!" he exclaimed in wonder. "Into the wagon with you, then, no questions asked. For by my troth, you're on the run, and misfortune shall befall us if we tarry."

Hans and Angela lay curled together under the wagon's heavy canopy, squeezed between baskets and boxes. The steady clip-clop of the horse's hooves and the gentle creak of the axles soothed their spirits. Soon they'd drifted into the deepest of dreamlands.

Hans found himself at a traveling circus. The ringmaster was a skeleton; the acrobats were rats in red-spangled tights. Meanwhile, Angela was having tea with Georgina von Hoffen-Toffen. "I didn't drown in a bath," Georgina simpered, "I drowned at sea. See how the fish ate my eyeballs?" An eel slithered in and out of her sockets, and every time she spoke a school of sardines swam out of her mouth.

By a curious coincidence, both dreamers heard the Necromancer say, "What have we here?" In Hans' dream, the ringmaster whipped a shroud around his shoulders and became the Evil One. Hans tried to escape, but the circus tent collapsed around him. A rat with Knobbe's face nuzzled his chin: "This will teach you to run from your papa."

In her neighboring dreamland, Angela hid behind her teacup as Georgina wiped the flesh from her skull. She was the Necromancer disguised in ringlets and a frock. Angela ran and bumped into a wall. All the windows and doors to the tearoom had disappeared.

The Necromancer smacked his lips. "Soon my pickling jars will be filled with fresh meat."

Hans and Angela cried out and awoke in the night, hearts pounding.

Angela clutched Hans. "I dreamed the Necromancer had us."

"So did I," Hans said. "But we're safe."

Angela held her breath. "Are we?"

"Aren't we?"

They were still in the back of the wagon, between the vegetables, herbs, and sundries. But something was different. The wagon had stopped moving. There was an eerie quiet. Hans wriggled to the front of the wagon. He lifted the cloth covering and looked to the driver's seat. It was empty.

"The peddler. He's gone."

Angela gulped. "He'll be back. . . . Won't he?"

"I don't think so," Hans said. "His horse is gone too. Another thing. We're not on the main road anymore. We're on a side trail."

"Why would the peddler abandon us in the middle of the forest?" Angela shivered. "Why would he leave us alone with his things?"

"Who says he had a choice? Who says we're alone?"

Quiet as a bedbug, Hans slid under the covering to the ground and motioned Angela to follow. They crouched low. The trail ahead was overgrown with vines and saplings. The wagon had been driven to the end of nowhere.

A nasty murmur floated through the air.

Hans took Angela's hand. "Weevils." He guided her over the roots of a large tree to the side of the path.

"Can they see us?" Angela whispered.

Something drifted behind them. Its long, scaly fingers

124

caressed their shoulders. "Oh yes, they can see you. I, too, in my way. For I hear you. Smell you. Feel you."

"Necromancer!" Hans and Angela swung their arms wildly.

"He's over here," mocked voices from the left. "No, over here," mocked voices from the right.

"No, here," said the Necromancer, raising a lantern window before their eyes. "My Weevils wanted to kill you in your sleep. I said to wait, the better to enjoy your terror. Was I right, my pets?"

"Yes, Master." A circle of lantern windows opened. Weevils were ringed around them, crows hopping at their feet.

"Take the grave robber's apprentice and the countess," the Necromancer said. "Prepare them for sacrifice."

The Weevils swarmed. One jumped on Hans' back. Three grabbed his arms, two yanked his legs, another pummeled his middle.

Angela thrust a hand into her treasure bag. "Take me or my jewels!" she cried, and threw a fistful of gems into the air. The Weevils squealed. For a second, they turned from their prey in search of the shinies.

Hans and Angela tore blindly into the forest night.

THE WOLF KING

"Don't let them escape!" the Necromancer shrieked.

The Weevils took after the pair with their lamps. "We sees you!" they taunted, as they hopped over stumps and ducked under branches. "We sees you!" They were so close their lanterns lit the way.

"Run faster," Hans panted. "They kill in packs." Fear spurred them on. Hans and Angela gained ground, but as they did the lamplight faded and they stumbled. The Weevils caught up.

"Pray God they tire," Angela gasped as they ran down a hillock.

"Pray, indeed," Hans said, for now, as well as the taunts of Weevils, the air was alive with the crow calls of the Necromancer.

In a flash, the night was a flapping of wings. The birds were everywhere—and everywhere invisible in the shadows, save for their cold, red eyes glinting in the lamplight. The Necromancer cawed again. The crows attacked with beak and claw.

"Shield your eyes!" Hans hollered. He drew his monk's hood tight; Angela pressed her helmet into her collar.

They tripped and tumbled forward. The crows landed on their backs, dug their talons into their shoulders. One pulled at Angela's hair, fallen from under her helmet; another pecked over her collar for her neck. Angela screamed.

The Weevils were nearly upon them. Hans and Angela struggled to their feet. Hans spotted a campfire through the trees ahead. "Help us!" he hollered to the clearing. "Help us." In a mad dash, he and Angela burst into the camp.

It was abandoned—emptied by some nightmare. Piles of bones circled the campsite, some old, some dripping blood and sinew.

"What hell is this?" Angela cried. "Is this where we're to die?"

The crows attacked again. They pecked and battered the pair to the ground. Hans and Angela curled into balls. The Weevils leaped on their backs. "We has you!"

127

The Necromancer's hollow laugh floated out of the forest. "Well done, my pets." He entered the clearing, spirited there by the grace of his crook and the second sight that lit his brain like the Evening Star. The crows flew to his feet. He tossed them a fistful of maggots.

"Treats for us, too, Master?" the Weevils begged.

"As many as you like, and shinies, too," the Necromancer said. "First, stake our prey to the ground." He turned to the warmth of the fire pit. "We seem to have scared off a band of poachers. Their flames will heat my blade."

Hans and Angela gripped their hands together. The Necromancer knelt between them. He pulled off Hans' hood and Angela's helmet and stroked their hair. "Be of good cheer. Your memory will live on. Your skins shall become the archduke's pillowcase and footstool, your insides stored in my pickling jars for spells."

"There is justice eternal for such as you," said Hans, as steadily as he could.

"Indeed," Angela said. "Even in tragedy, villains end badly. Ask anyone."

"I write my own story, little one," the Necromancer said. "At the moment, we're on the page where you die."

From beyond the clearing, a wolf howled. A second. A third. A fourth. The Weevils looked up. Heavy paws bounded through the forest around them. Fur flashed between the trees. A wolf pack emerged at the edges of the campsite: a pack as large as it was lean.

The crows flew into the branches. A Weevil tugged on the Necromancer's shroud. "What shall we do, Master?"

"Wolves fear fire; they'll stay at bay," the Necromancer said. "When we're done, we'll toss them a few limbs from our little friends."

Unearthly roars shook the night beyond the thicket of bushes past the fire pit: roars so strange and mutant they could only come from monsters of myth and legend. The Weevils squealed.

"Strangers, begone!" a voice boomed.

The Necromancer smiled. "We are on business of His Royal Highness Arnulf, Archduke of Waldland. You and your fellows would be wise to flee, on peril of your lives."

"We are no 'fellows,' nor take we orders from mortals," the voice roared. "Know ye that I am the Wolf King. Behold my monster horde."

Monstrous heads of fang and fur reared above the tallest bushes. Their eyes gleamed fire. Thunder rumbled the cloudless night.

The terrified Weevils leaped off Hans and Angela and pressed themselves at the Necromancer's feet. Hans and Angela jumped up, but escape was impossible. Wolves circled all round and monsters howled beyond the thicket.

The Necromancer cocked his head. He could hear the animals and the thunder, smell the fur and blood, and knew that the creatures were taller than carnival freaks. Yet something was not as it seemed.

He sniffed through his bony noseholes and flicked the air with his lizard tongue. "I, too, can conjure thunder from thin air, Wolf King," he said. "Yea, and have creatures to do my bidding. Before we speak further, I should like my crows to investigate your monsters." He craned his neck and cawed three times.

The crows flew from their branches. They circled the campsite twice and swooped toward the Wolf King's bushes. Yet before they could cross the clearing, they were pierced by a wave of blazing arrows. Their feathers burst into flame; they shrieked to the ground in fiery spirals.

The wolves went wild at the smell of blood. They tore into the circle to rip at the fallen birds. As the pack charged, the Weevils screamed off into the forest.

"Come back," the Necromancer commanded. "I order you back!" But they were gone.

Hans grabbed Angela's hand. "Time for us to go, too."

"No! Not now!"

The Necromancer spun to their voices. He flailed his crook on the ground around them. "You, boy. You, girl. Do you think to escape me?" But the night was so thick with sounds, smells, tastes, and dangers—his senses so flooded—that he was all but truly blind. He reached into his shroud and held aloft a bag of powder.

"Apprentice! Countess! We'll meet again!" he cried. "As for you, Wolf King: I'll see you and your monster horde in Hell!"

He threw the powder into the fire pit. There was a huge explosion. A billow of smoke. And in that smoke, the Necromancer vanished into the night.

24
WARRIORS OF THE IMAGINATION

*H*ans and Angela faced the monstrous heads that loomed above the thicket. All around, wolves licked their bloody fangs and howled.

"Did you not hear my dread command?" the Wolf King roared. "Begone or face my wrath."

"Sorry for disturbing Your Majesty," Hans gulped. "We'll be on our way."

"We most certainly will not," Angela said.

"Then your deaths shall be savage and strange," the Wolf King boomed.

"Far less savage and strange than what awaits us out there with the Necromancer and his Weevils," Angela said.

"Next to them, to be torn apart by monsters and wolves would be a relief."

"Come behind this thicket and say that," the Wolf King sneered. Laughter rose from the monster horde.

"No," Angela tossed back. "If you plan to eat us, have the courage to eat us in the clearing."

"You question our courage? We who fear neither mortal nor beast?"

Hans blanched. "Angela, apologize or they'll kill us."

"Heed the wisdom of your protector," the Wolf King warned.

"Him?" Angela rolled her eyes. "He's only a grave rob-ber's apprentice. I, on the other hand, am Countess Angela Gabriela von Schwanenberg. I've outwitted the great Archduke Arnulf and escaped the grave, so I have no idea why I should tremble and quake before a ragtag gaggle of cowardly fiends who hide behind bushes."

Three of the monsters belched fire. Hans prepared for the worst.

"Have you not seen our flaming arrows?" boomed the Wolf King.

"A quick and merciful death they'd provide. But that's hardly the horrible end you've advertised. So come: Brandish your claws. Do your worst. I dare you."

A roll of thunder. The wolves covered their ears with their paws.

Angela yawned. "I'm sorry, but I don't believe you're a Wolf King or that you have any monsters. Still, you put on a wonderful show with your pet wolves and fire breathers. You ought to perform in village squares on May Day."

A third peal of thunder shook the night. "What of my power over the heavens?" the Wolf King demanded.

"Oh, that," Angela said. "I own a thunder sheet myself. It came with my puppet theater. I've found it very useful in producing sound effects for storms. Mine is a thin sheet of bronze with a cushioned velvet trim to protect my fingers when I shake it. Yours, I imagine, is cheap scrap metal."

The heads of the monster horde reared high. Hans gasped.

"I know about stick puppets, too," Angela continued. "Those monstrous heads are surely crafted from beasts you've hunted for food. Theirs are the bones that litter your campsite. You put red lanterns in the skulls to create the fiery eyes, and add painted wooden horns and tusks by means of glue and leather bindings. Then you attach the heads to poles so you can make them soar and tower. I also expect you're all on horseback so that your roars seem to come from the puppets' jaws."

"You think my creatures are puppets?" the Wolf King exclaimed in outrage.

Hans smacked his forehead with delight. "But of course! It's what the Necromancer couldn't sense, and what his

Weevils and I could never imagine."

"Why should a lord of the underworld play with the toys of mortal children?" the Wolf King thundered.

Hans threw up a hand like a student who'd solved his teacher's prize riddle. "When Papa robbed the graves of Wottenberg, I pretended we were ghosts to frighten locals out of the cemetery. He dug undisturbed an entire summer, while I shook a sack of chains and moaned from mausoleums. You're the same: highwaymen who scare people away from the forest so you can rob at will!"

Angela grinned. "Congratulations, Sir So-called Wolf King. Even I, well-versed in the art of puppetry, was fooled at first."

The monster heads looked at each other, then came from behind the bushes, carried by eight sheepish men on horseback. The riders wore grubby velvet doublets and torn linen leggings under patched woolen knee breeches; their faces and hands were smeared with soot. They circled Hans and Angela, and dismounted. The wolves wagged their tails and frisked around them.

The "Wolf King" stepped forward. He was a little man as delicate as a lark, except for an Adam's apple the size of a walnut. "Intelligence is a dangerous gift. Now that you know our secret, what are we to do with you?"

"Show us the quickest path to the mountain home of Peter the Hermit," Angela said brightly.

"Why should we let you free to reveal our secret?" the little man asked.

An excellent question. Hans summoned the finest court talk he could imagine. "Because you're good and decent thieves who'd never harm sworn enemies of the archduke," he said heroically. "The proof? You rob the ill-gotten gains of the idle rich, not the hard-earned coin of the honest poor."

Angela shot him a look. As a countess, she wasn't sure she liked this line of reasoning. "You're also men of kind and tender hearts," she said. "You could have slain the Necromancer and his Weevils with your arrows. Instead you merely killed his crows, and only when attacked."

The little man puffed out his chest in indignation. "How dare you call us good and decent, kind and tender? We're ruffians. Savage ruffians. We let the archduke's wizard and his gang escape to spread our legend."

"So will we, if you set us free beyond the forest," Hans replied. "We're hunted too. We'd never betray you."

"Besides, we share another bond," Angela said "We're Artists: Keepers of the Divine Flame! Warriors of the Imagination." Angela couldn't remember where she'd read the line, but it had the desired effect.

"You think I'm an artist?" The little man's Adam's apple bobbed up and down like a bird at a rain barrel.

"Upon my word," Angela declared. "Who else could

inspire tavern songs that terrify an archduchy?"

The little man stomped on his hat. "I'm *more* than an inspiration! I'm the poet who penned those ballads! But who gets the credit? Anonymous!"

"How tragic for you to labor in obscurity," Angela declared. "You, whose verses are the finest in the archduchy!"

"The finest in the archduchy?" His lower lip wobbled. "You're the first to ever say so."

"The world is a hard place for artists," Angela said solemnly. "A young countess, now deceased, once called my puppet plays childish and silly."

"The very words that sent me packing from three châteaus and a barony. Oh, such critics *deserve* to die," he wept. "Know, then, my true name, kindred spirit. I am Tomas Bundt, Esquire, Artist and Poet Extraordinaire. The *Tomas* is spelled without an *h*." He bowed low, brushing the ground with the brim of his battered buckram hat. "My men are musicians cast from court for playing my wedding serenades. Mocked by nobles of little soul and less taste, we repaired to the great forest, where we have pursued our Muse, taking vengeance on those who abused us."

A large gray wolf nuzzled his breeches. "Let me introduce Siegfried, the truest friend that ever lived." He let the beast lick his face. "At first, we feared the wolf pack and tossed it meat to spare ourselves. Such feeding made us their boon companions. Thanks to them and our monster heads, we never need to draw a pistol. One look, and nobles run screaming from their carriages."

Hans placed his hand over his heart. "Tomas Bundt, Esquire, Artist and Poet Extraordinaire: Take us to the mountain of Peter the Hermit, and when our tale is done, you shall be immortalized for helping to save the Little Countess from the forces of darkness."

Before Tomas could say a word, Siegfried and his pack began to run in circles, sniffing the air. Now the rest could smell it, too. Smoke. It drifted across the campsite from little fires in the underbrush circling the clearing.

"The Necromancer!" Hans exclaimed. "He's returned to burn us alive."

"We've no time to lose," Tomas said. He and his men jumped onto their horses.

"What about us?" Angela cried.

"The Wolf King will never forsake a fellow artist, nor a good-hearted outlaw," Tomas promised. "Hop aboard."

Hans cupped his hands. Angela sprang from the foot-hold to a seat behind Tomas. One leap, and Hans was safely at her back. Tomas and his men spurred their horses and burst through the billowing smoke into the clear night air.

"The Necromancer will follow our scent," Angela said.

"Fear not," Tomas replied. "A scent can be tracked over ground, not through water. We'll gallop to one of a dozen nearby streams and get you to the base of your hermit's mountain by daybreak."

ACT III

Peter the Hermit

25
THE FROZEN TOMB

*T*rue to his word, Tomas Bundt got Hans and Angela to the hermit's mountain by sunrise. The snow-capped peak towered without end, the hermitage appearing no bigger than a speck of pepper on a pillowcase.

Hans and Angela shared a hearty breakfast with the outlaws: dried sausage and drier bread, washed down with river water fed from the mountain's springs. Siegfried bounded up with a stick, laid it at Hans' feet, and wagged his tail. Hans grinned and tossed it. The beast fetched and bounded back.

"You've found a new friend," Tomas smiled.

Hans scratched the great wolf's ears. "Angela and I have to go now, Siegfried. We have a good day's climb if we're to reach the hermitage by nightfall." Siegfried raised a paw as if to shake good-bye.

The outlaws gathered round. Tomas presented Hans with a pair of boots. "You'll need these to keep your feet from freezing on the upper slope. I stole them from a cruel magistrate to make him walk in the steps of the barefoot poor."

"Thank you from the bottom of my heart," Hans said. "These are the first boots I've ever had. The first shoes, even."

"May they keep your feet as warm as your heart," Tomas said.

Angela shook his hand. "Fair thee well, Tomas Bundt, Esquire, Poet and Wolf King Extraordinaire." She removed the three remaining jewels from her treasure bag. "Take these for your help and kindness. They're all that I have, though less than you deserve."

Tomas was overwhelmed. "In truth, I deserve nothing. Despite my airs, I'm neither Wolf King nor Poet, but a storybook of lies."

Angela shook her head. "Truth is made of such stories. Without your Wolf King, we'd have perished at the Necromancer's hands. Yet here we stand, alive and well. What truer tale is there than that?"

"Thank you," Tomas said. His Adam's apple bobbled up his throat.

"I, too, would like to show my thanks," said Hans, "but I have nothing with which to repay you."

Tomas looked into the bright eyes of the young apprentice. "Remember me," Tomas said. "There is no greater gift than that."

Hans and Angela climbed all day. They began on a footpath that ran along a stream. There were berry bushes and cows grazing on lush grasses; the bells on their necks provided dull melodies in the breeze.

By midafternoon, they reached a stream that gushed from the mountainside. From here, the path zigzagged as the route grew steeper. The grasses were shorter, the earth stripped from the stone. Mountain goats cocked their heads as if wondering if Hans and Angela had gifts of bread and cheese.

The air grew crisp to the skin. Hans rubbed his hands against the cold.

Angela paused. "Would you like my gloves?"

"I'm fine," Hans said. "You keep warm." He blew into his palms and snuck them up the sleeves of his robe. "We'd better move fast if we're to reach the hermitage by dusk."

Angela nodded and pulled her general's helmet over her ears. They had climbed so high that frost covered the rocks in shadow.

The trail ended. From here, a rough stack of stone

shelves rose into the heights. They mounted some of the shelves like stairs. Others were over their heads. For these, Angela crawled onto Hans' shoulders and wrestled herself up; then he'd jump high and use her dangling arms as climbing ropes.

The shelves grew more treacherous, lined with crusted snow. Pellets and chunks fell inside their boots and melted against their feet and ankles. The wet leather was useless against the cold, and soon too rigid to grip the rock. Angela slipped. Hans grabbed her by the elbow. His hands were turning blue.

The sun dropped behind the mountains. The route ahead was uncertain, the light dim, the shadows deep.

"We'll never make the hermitage in the dark," Hans shivered. "One wrong move, and we'll fall to our deaths. Two shelves up and over there's a crevice big enough to hold us. We'll rest there till daybreak."

"No," Angela said, teeth chattering. "We'll freeze to death."

"Not if we huddle together."

Hans pushed her to the next ledge and crawled up after. Clouds curled around them. The crevice drifted out of sight. Hans hoisted himself to the final grade, and reached down. Angela grabbed his arms through the icy mist. Hans pulled long and hard. At last she was beside him.

They sat panting with exhaustion, their backs to the

frigid rock, their legs dangling over the precipice.

"The crevice is to our left," Hans said. They slid across, inch by inch, and pressed themselves inside. The wind whistled around them.

"If anything happens to me," Angela said quietly, "I want you to know you're my best friend in the whole world. In fact, you're my only friend ever."

"You're mine, too," Hans said, and held her tight. "But nothing's going to happen to you. I promise."

He knew it was a lie. They couldn't survive. But in the crevice they'd die in peace, not in pieces. He couldn't bear the thought of Angela's screams as she tumbled down the mountain, or of her body smashed and battered. Nor did he fancy the same for himself. "We're in this together," he whispered into her ear. "Friends to the end."

"Yes," Angela whispered back. "Friends to the end."

She couldn't feel her feet. Her face was numb. She closed her eyes and saw her mother and father. If she were to die, they'd be lost forever. She had to survive for them. She opened her eyes quickly. They closed again. She blinked and struggled to keep them open. But the cold was too much. They closed, closed, slowly, and she was still.

Hans kissed her gently on the forehead. The crevice was a different kind of tomb than any he'd entered before. At least he'd be free in the fresh air, not trapped in a box.

Ice crystals formed on his lashes; they flickered shut.

The numbness in his limbs felt warm, so warm—and for a moment, he dreamed that a kindly man was wrapping him in a blanket. "Courage, my son." The lid of a box closed over him. Then he flew through the air, there was a great splash, and a rocking in the pitch-black.

Hans heard the voice again.

"Courage. Courage. We're nearly there."

His lids flickered open. There was a great light. He and Angela were rising into it. All around them, men in white were rising alongside.

"He's coming round!" the voice rang out.

Hans turned to the sound and found his face buried in a world of whiskers. He leaned back and saw a ruddy-faced man with a bushy white beard and a shock of white hair that bloomed in all directions. A halo of light glowed through the tangled mane.

"Are you God?" Hans asked in wonder.

"No," the man laughed. "I'm Peter the Hermit."

26

RESTING WITH THE DEAD

At that very moment, the Necromancer reentered the abandoned cemetery, alone and hungry. He'd eaten the carrots he'd taken from the peddler's wagon. Now there were only two potatoes left to gnaw on. These he'd stored in his empty sockets. *After all,* he mused grimly, *potatoes have eyes.*

He picked his way to Hans and Angela's old coffin tunnel. *Where is my prey now?* he wondered. *What will I tell the archduke when I return to Castle Schwanenberg?*

The Necromancer knelt down by the hole. Where better to think and dream than cocooned in the dank earth? He slithered inside and lay very still. Worms came out of the tunnel walls and wriggled up his shroud. He relaxed as they crawled over his arms and legs. *What peace,* he thought, *to rest with corpses.*

His mind drifted to the moment of Hans and Angela's escape. He knew there was no Wolf King nor monster horde: Magical creatures had no need for horses. Clearly, that meant the fellows were outlaws, using disguise to frighten the world from their hideaway. Harmless, too, or they'd have killed him and his Weevils, not just his crows.

So why had they taken the boy and the girl? Not for reward: The children could expose them. And not for slaughter: They could have killed the brats in the clearing. That left but one explanation: They were escorting them somewhere.

But why? Out of kindness? If the Necromancer had had eyes, he would have rolled them. Good-hearted thieves, like garrulous nurses and evil wizards, were the stuff of fairy tales.

Besides, the only important question was *where.* The place must be secluded, for no town could provide safe haven from his spies. And it was surely in the north, for north was the only direction they'd traveled. Indeed, *far* north, the peddler's wagon suggesting a long journey.

But where in the far north could they find sanctuary?

A slug poked its moist horns into the Necromancer's left earhole, as if confiding a secret.

"Ah." The Necromancer smiled. "But of course!"

27

PETER THE HERMIT

*A*ll night, Hans drifted in and out of consciousness. He was aware of a room built of rocks and mortar, and of smoke drifting up from a stone hearth to a blackened timber ceiling. The air smelled of eucalyptus. A few of the hermits warmed his hands and feet with its oil and made him breathe over a steaming pot of pine needles. They laid him before the hearth under a pile of goat hides. Angela was nearby under a second pile.

Peter the Hermit sat between them. He stroked their hair, wiped the sweat from their brows with rags, and raised their heads so they could drink a bitter tea of roots and bark. All the while, he whispered encouragement and prayers.

The other hermits ringed the room singing in Latin. Some knelt on the ground, heads rolled back, palms extended upward. Others twirled in a circle, white robes billowing around them.

"Is this the hermitage?" Hans murmured.

Peter squeezed his hand. "It's home," he said. "Wherever you are is home."

Their fevers broke before dawn; by noon, they were propped up slurping chicken broth from tankards. The other hermits were off on their daily chores. Peter had stayed behind, their health his sole concern.

Hans marveled at their host. He was dressed in leather motley with a patchwork cloak that swept from his broad shoulders over his muscular arms and chest. A man of all seasons, his broad face and hands were worn by the sun, while his bright, blue eyes pierced the gloom like a harbor lamp. Most striking of all was his spectacular shock of hair and beard. It looked like a nesting ground for sparrows.

Hans tried not to stare. "How did you know where to find us?"

"The lookout spotted you at midday," Peter said. "We watched you climb through our telescope, uncertain if you were friend or foe. When it got dark, we decided to act. It's much more agreeable fetching live bodies than dead ones."

Angela took a glug of her soup. "Why do you have a lookout?"

"Aren't you happy that we *do*?" Peter smiled.

Angela scrunched her nose. "Is that an answer?"

"It's the one you're getting," Peter laughed. "But here are a couple of questions for *you*: Who are you? Why are you here?"

"Well, to begin, I'm Countess Angela Gabriela von Schwanenberg, and this is my best friend, Hans."

"Angela Gabriela von Schwanenberg," Peter said with a start. "I gave you your name. Your mother and father let me sleep in your haymow."

"Yes," Angela said, "and now I've come to seek sanctuary with you. The archduke has imprisoned my parents; he seeks our deaths."

"What?"

Angela told him their tale, Peter shaking his head and rocking as the occasion required. When she described her burial, he leaped from his stool. When she spoke of her rescue by Hans, he gave the lad a fatherly hug. "Blessèd be the grave robbers!"

"I'm just an apprentice." Hans blushed.

"To return to the point," Angela said crisply, "my parents say you're wise. I need you to tell me how to rescue them."

"First, you must rest," Peter replied. "No child fresh

from her deathbed is fit to confront the power of the archduke and his necromancer."

"But time is short. My parents are in danger."

"Time is never so short as life itself."

Angela kicked her foot under the covers. "You don't understand. How can you? The archduke's never harmed you."

"No?" The color drained from Peter's cheeks. "That villain caused the death of my son. My only child."

"I'm sorry," Angela said. "I didn't know."

The hermit's eyes filled with tears. "My wife had passed away in childbirth. When I lost my child as well, I wandered the land, unhinged by grief. That's how I came upon your parents. They restored my mind and I retreated here, far from the horrors of the world." He blinked. "I grow tiresome. Come, bundle yourselves and step to the porch."

The porch of the great hall was constructed of thick planks resting on small stone pillars. From here, Hans and Angela looked over the hermitage grounds. It was a large, triangular plateau: One side, a hundred yards wide, marked the mountain face on which they'd nearly died. The other two sides backed onto a steep V-shaped slope that towered to the mountain's summit.

"This porch is our altar," Peter said reverently, "the plateau our chapel."

Hans was awestruck. Sheltered on three sides, but open

to the southern sun, the plateau was like a meadow in early spring. A few sheep and goats munched on hardy grasses; daffodils, crocuses, and bluebells poked through clumps of snow at the base of berry bushes; and the inner walls of the mountain were covered in moss and evergreens.

Angela pointed at the hermits. They were standing around a large tree stump at the center of the grounds. Each held a heavy wooden sword and took turns attacking the stump with thrusts and roars.

"They're pell training!" Angela exclaimed.

"It's their daily exercise," Peter said.

"But pell training is what knights do before tournaments and battle."

"Knights are what they were, the sons of noble families, before grief brought them to this mountain as it brought me."

"Where did they come from?" Hans asked.

"From as far away as it took them to get here," Peter said.

Angela rolled her eyes at Hans: A hermit speaking in riddles was as irritating in real life as it was in storybooks. As mysterious, too.

Peter combed his fingers through his hair. His mood brightened. "Our stump is one of the finest pells around. You're welcome to train when you're able."

"I'd love to," Hans said.

"I'd rather not perspire if I don't have to," Angela said. "But I'll need to do something till I'm well enough to rescue my parents. At home, I made puppets. Do you have a workshop?"

Peter pointed across the plateau. "We make wine barrels and caskets in that barn over there. Use whatever tools you wish."

Hans saw a series of carved openings in the rock wall behind the barn. "What's in those holes?"

"They're hermit cells, where we contemplate by day and sleep by night. We'll prepare one for each of you."

"I've spent my life in a cave," Hans said. "Could we please sleep in the great hall instead?"

"Unchaperoned?" Peter raised his bushy eyebrows. "What would your parents say to that?" he asked Angela in amusement.

"They'd say one of us should stay in the main building, the other in the barn. And since I'm a girl and a countess, well . . ." She smiled at Hans.

"Fine," Hans grumped. "I'll take the barn. If it gets too cold, I guess I can cuddle up to the sheep."

Peter patted him on the back. "Good lad." He began to lead them back inside.

"Wait," Angela said. "What's that hidden by the pines up the mountain?"

Peter paused. "My private chapel. The one place you

must never go. Never, on pain of banishment."

"Why?"

Peter's eyes flashed. "Because I say so." He turned abruptly and marched across the grounds. Hans and Angela watched him in stunned silence.

"Banishment?" Angela frowned. "Why is the chapel so important?"

"I don't know and I don't intend to find out."

"But it's all so strange. Who was Peter before he became a hermit? Why did Arnulf kill his son? And what are the secrets hidden in his chapel?"

"One thing's certain," Hans said. "Peter the Hermit is not what he seems."

28

TALL TALES

*T*he Necromancer arrived in County Schwanenberg at dusk. He expected his Weevils would be hiding in Potter's Field, while the archduke would be pacing the castle halls, impatiently punching holes in the stonework. Instead, he found the Weevils sitting cross-legged in the courtyard, decked out in new finery—frock coats and breeches, sewn by village dressmakers from the von Schwanenberg family tapestries. Arnulf was entertaining them with a puppet play starring his hand bones.

At the sight of the Necromancer, the Weevils fell at his feet, touched the hem of his shroud, and kissed his scaly toes. "We thought you wuz dead, Master. We thought them wolves and monsters had eated you up."

"You thought wrong, my pets."

"High Chancellor," Arnulf exclaimed, "I'm delighted you survived. Your Weevils told me of the Wolf King's assault and of their brave pursuit of the grave robber's apprentice and the countess."

The Necromancer craned his head to the Weevils. "Tell me of this pursuit, my pets, for you left me in the clearing."

The eldest thrust out his chin. "When the Wolf King's pack attacked, our prey runned into the woods. We runned after 'em and killed 'em dead."

The Necromancer smiled. "Where, pray tell, are the bodies?"

"The monsters flew down and ate 'em," the Weevil said solemnly. "Then they flied away, leaving us only the heart of the boy."

"Your Weevils presented it to me," Arnulf said, "along with the girl's bloody burial jewels. In reward, I've made them knights of the realm."

"Sir Weevils? Oh my." The Necromancer feigned a bow and stroked their cheeks with his fingernails. "How quickly they grow up," he sighed to Arnulf. "No longer my gang of pets, but little men who curry favor to advance themselves."

"Yes, Master," said a Weevil with scabby knuckles. "Soon we'll be as powerful at court as you. Even more, for we has eyes to see."

There was a dangerous pause. "You may have eyes," the Necromancer said drily, "yet, sadly, you are blind."

"Blind?"

"Yes, blind to the danger of seeking to steal my power. Blind to the peril of betraying the archduke with lies."

"What?" Arnulf exclaimed.

"No. We never lied," the Weevils quaked.

"You lie even now," the Necromancer continued. "You fled the Wolf King's beasts like cowards and left me to face the foe alone. Then you stole the heart from the peddler I killed and dipped the girl's burial jewels in the muck."

Arnulf whirled on the Weevils. "Explain yourselves."

The Weevils froze. "It were a story. An innocent story."

"Whoever heard of an innocent story?" the Necromancer scoffed. "Those who control stories control the world."

"What shall we do with the traitors?" the archduke asked.

The Necromancer clasped his hands in prayer. "Spare the rod and spoil the child," he said piously.

"Indeed," Arnulf thundered. "May your fate be a tale of sound moral instruction." He snatched the Weevils two at a time and crashed them together like cymbals. The Necromancer rubbed his tummy: Their little skulls reminded him of eggs being cracked for an omelet. That is, if eggs screamed.

Arnulf tossed the Weevils into a pile. "I trust I didn't go too far?"

"Heavens, no. One must be cruel only to be kind."

"Well said." Arnulf flexed his iron knuckles. "So to business: What *really* happened to the boy and girl?"

"The Wolf King's creatures flew them to safety," the Necromancer said, weaving a cunning yarn of his own. "Yet victory shall still be yours, Excellency, for these winged monsters are mere warlocks who change their shape at will."

"How do you know?"

"Last night I lay with the dead. My spirit flew above the earth and found the monsters with the children, returning to human form."

"We'll hunt them down and mount their heads in my throne room," Arnulf exulted. "But who are they? Where do they live?"

"Come to the crypt," the Necromancer said. "I'll show you in a vision."

"At once." Arnulf grabbed a lantern and motioned his guards to follow.

The instant the courtyard was empty, two tiny Weevils peeked out from under the pile of their brethren.

"Is we still alive?" whispered one.

"I thinks so," the other whispered back.

"So what does we do now?"

"We runs. We runs where Master will never think to find us."

Arnulf followed the Necromancer through the grove to the von Schwanenberg family tomb. He posted his guards at a distance, and entered the crypt. Something otherworldly always swirled about the Necromancer, but here, surrounded by centuries of the dead, Arnulf felt ghosts in the very air he breathed.

The Necromancer tapped Angela's coffin with his staff and traced a hexagon around it. "Lie in the girl's death chamber."

Arnulf placed his lantern at the foot of the coffin and crawled inside. The Necromancer took a musky fungus from a pouch and placed it on the archduke's tongue. At once, the room spun before Arnulf's eyes. He rolled to his side and fell back sweating; his pupils vibrated wildly.

The Necromancer circled him, crablike; he tilted his head above the archduke's. Lamplight danced in his empty sockets. "What do you see?"

"Caverns, caves," the archduke moaned.

"Yes," the Necromancer sang in a faraway voice. "The warlocks live in little caves. Can you see them at their magic?"

The archduke stared hard into the shadowy sockets.

Yes, yes, he imagined, *there they are, little shadow-men flitting about the caves.*

The Necromancer slithered to Arnulf's feet. "Look above you. Can you see them flying the night sky?"

Arnulf stared up at the flickering shapes that darted about the ceiling. The more he stared, the more he saw creatures, like the Necromancer said—monsters with wings and tails that vanished the instant they appeared. It was like staring at cloud-shapes, only dark and frightening and real. "Where do they land?"

"Look around you," the Necromancer prodded. "The dead will guide you. Let your eyes climb up into the clouds."

Arnulf did as he was told. He watched the lamplight scale the shelves of coffins, ledge by ledge, to the flickering shapes on the ceiling. The banks of coffins, they were like . . . *mountains?* he wondered. "They're in the mountains!" he gasped.

"Yes, Excellency," the Necromancer murmured. He led Arnulf's mind forward. "The creatures land in the far mountains, where they return to human form."

"But nobody lives in the far mountains. Nobody except a few hermits."

The Necromancer let the thought float in the air.

Arnulf blinked in amazement. "The hermits are warlocks?"

The Necromancer remained silent; the thought took hold.

"What a clever disguise!" Arnulf exclaimed, his eyes as big as breastplates. "The warlocks live in the clouds, yes, where they change into hermits without being seen!"

"You're wise, Excellency, and cunning," the Necromancer flattered. "The hermitage in the far mountains with its little caves, that's where they've taken the boy and girl. That's where you shall slay them."

Arnulf frowned. "What if the hermits turn back into monsters?"

The Necromancer recalled an old legend. "From ancient times, mirrored shields have subdued such creatures; they freeze at the sight of their ugliness."

Arnulf wiped the sweat from his brow. "We must return to the palace immediately. I'll raise some troops and forge those mirrored shields. By week's end, we'll be at the warlocks' lair, where I'll slaughter the Wolf King and his monsters. There'll be epic songs and poems. My name will live forever. And you, dear friend, will have treasure without end!"

"Many thanks." The Necromancer smiled slyly. With no more than a lantern, a crypt, and a pinch of dried mushroom, he'd bound the archduke to him with the most powerful magic of all: Imagination.

29

THE FORBIDDEN CHAPEL

By the following morning, Hans and Angela were fit enough to explore the hermitage grounds. Peter gave them new warm clothes to replace the tattered robe and general's coat and led them to the cliff edge. Below, the river and mountain streams were squiggles of thread glittering in the sun.

"The proper way up is to follow the goat trails on the sides," Peter said. "It's hard going, but at least you'll get here alive."

Snow swept down the sloping rock face on the right side of the cliff edge before disappearing as it circled the mountain. "The shadows from the western cliffs keep it from melting. It makes for a quick ride down, but I wouldn't advise it," Peter said. "I once skidded two hundred yards on my backside before grabbing a passing berry bush. I nearly died of fright."

A heavy bell rang out. The hermits ran from their cells brandishing their wooden swords and circled the tree stump at the center of the grounds.

"Pell training!" Peter exclaimed.

"That's my cue to explore your workshop," Angela said, as she backed away from the rock face.

"And mine to have fun," Hans grinned. He and Peter made their way to the pell. "Why are the swords made of wood? And why strike at a wooden stump?"

"The wooden swords are twice as heavy as metal ones. If war ever comes, a real sword will feel light as a feather," Peter said. "The pell is useful too. You can strike at a post in ways that would kill a friend in practice."

Hans took to the pell as a duck to water. Years of digging and hauling had given him strength, while tunneling had made him agile. A special thrill was the freedom to roar as he charged.

Even better was the chance to try his hand at the quarterstaff and longstaff. The staves were made of oak and hawthorn. The quarterstaff was eight feet in length; the longstaff, fifteen. Peter taught him how to place one hand at the center of the staff and the other halfway to the end. Soon he was parrying thrusts and upending opponents with a sweep behind their knees.

Hans had used his shovel like this to defend himself against Knobbe. But he was astonished at the extra power that came with the staff's extra length, and the steadiness it required for control. More than once he found himself on the ground surrounded by laughing hermits.

"I learned the sidestep, duck, dodge and slip, and how to trap and jam a sword and staff," he enthused to Angela over goat stew. She smiled and nodded the way polite people do when totally bored. Asked about her morning, she shrugged and looked away. It was peculiar, but Hans had no time for questions. After lunch, it was time to train with kite shield and buckler.

The week flew by, Hans practicing battle arts while Angela did who-knew-what in the workshop. On the seventh day, a blizzard deposited a blanket of snow on the hermitage and down the far right slope of the mountain. The hermits marveled at Hans' ability to keep his footing in the slippery slush.

"Where did you learn such balance?" Peter asked.

"From sloshing about in muddy graves." Hans blushed.

The afternoon following the storm, Angela was sitting on a rock by the cliff edge peering down at a bank of clouds that had rolled in before dawn. When the hermits left to meditate, Hans came over and sat beside her. She didn't look up.

"It looks like a giant's duvet," Hans said to break the silence.

"Uh-huh," she said absently.

Hans studied her frown. "What's the matter?"

"Nothing."

"Tell me. For days you've barely said a word. Why? What's going on?"

Angela drew into herself. "I've seen things I shouldn't. Don't make me say what. It's for your own good."

"Says who?"

"I have to go." She went to stand up.

Hans held her by the arm. "Not till you tell me your secret. We're friends: Friends to the end, remember?"

Angela looked from Hans to the hermit cells and back again. "All right. But don't say I didn't warn you." She took a breath. "I've been inside Peter's chapel."

Hans gasped. "He said we mustn't go there!"

"Exactly. Forbidden places are always the most interesting. Anyway, no one was watching. You were all too busy hitting that stupid stump. So I snuck into the pine trees and made my way up to the chapel. It wasn't locked or anything."

"Of course not," Hans said. "This is a place of trust. What would you have done if Peter had caught you?"

"I'd have cried and said I was sorry and how I was just looking for a chisel to make a puppet head."

"How stupid. He said he'd banish us."

"He'd never banish *me*. I'm a girl and a countess and he gave me my name. *You* he might, though. Life is unfair for girls, but sometimes for boys, too; especially poor boys. That's why I didn't tell you. Because what I saw is so strange, I knew if I told, you'd want to see for yourself."

"See *what*?"

"All sorts of things. Maps. A foreign crest. A hidden cave—"

"A hidden cave?"

Angela nodded. "The chapel is built over a hole in the rock that leads into a cave in the mountain. The cave is filled with boxes of old tunics, chain mail, and battle gear: two-handed swords, rapiers, falchions, poniards, and daggers. At the back are wooden stairs that lead out of the top of the cave onto the slope above the chapel. There on a ledge, hidden by trees and boulders, is a giant catapult."

Hans whistled. "A catapult? There's nothing to fire at but air."

"I told you, it's strange."

"And the maps and the foreign crest?" Hans asked.

"One of the maps is of Market Square in the capital," Angela said. "It has a dotted line showing the catacombs under the square that connect the palace to the cathedral.

Other maps, equally detailed, are of the city and country-side. And one last map is the answer to my prayers. It holds the key to rescuing my parents."

"What is it?"

"A detailed plan of the inside of the palace," Angela said. "There are drawings of floor upon floor as well as red markings that could be secret passageways. There's also the plan of an underground dungeon with a lagoon to the outside. Hans, that map can lead me to Mother and Father."

"How could a hermit have a map of the palace?" Hans asked gently.

"It doesn't matter."

"It does." Hans squeezed her hand. "Palace maps are secret. No one knows the archduke's private passageways. The map may *look* real, Angela, but it's invented by the same mind that built a catapult to nowhere."

"Not everything in the chapel is pretend," Angela fought back. "There's the battle gear. . . ."

"Yes," Hans said. "Brought here by the hermits from their former lives and put in storage. That's not the same as a map to your parents' cell."

Angela's eyes misted. "I know it seems impossible. But what if it's not? What if Peter has secrets beyond our understanding? It's not just the maps—even the foreign crest looks real."

"Anyone can make up a crest."

"Yes, but this one's so bold I can still see it: Two dancing unicorns. Above them, lightning bolts flying from an eagle's head—"

Hans went pale. "Angela, don't play tricks on me."

"I'm not."

"The unicorns—are they dancing on a bed of wreaths?"

"Yes," Angela said. "With zephyrs blowing from the left."

"And the sun shining from the right?"

"How did you know?"

"That crest. It's carved in the chest that floated me to shore. Angela, I have to see it. Now."

30

AN ASTONISHING DISCOVERY

As Hans and Angela raced to Peter's chapel, fifty of the archduke's men were scaling the hermits' peak with mirrored shields. All morning, they'd climbed the goat paths under cover of cloud. Now, as the sky cleared, they were within reach of the plateau. Arnulf observed them through a telescope from his position at the base of the mountain.

The Necromancer lounged by his side, little mirrors fitted to his eye sockets. "Soon your men will fell those warlock-hermits with sword and arrow, and toss their bodies from the cliff," he cooed.

"Except for the boy and girl," Arnulf gloated. "They

shall burn as witches in Market Square. Their screams will terrify the world till doomsday."

Hans and Angela took Peter's trail to the chapel, keeping their steps within his to cover their tracks. They knew they didn't have much time; the hermits' meditations would soon be over. Hans lifted the latch; the door creaked open; they slid inside.

Hans took a deep breath. It felt odd being where he shouldn't, like his nights in graveyards. Even odder was the knowledge that this chapel might hold the key to the puzzle of his past.

Angela led Hans to the wall with the crest. Its images emerged like figures from a dream: the unicorns, the zephyrs, the Latin words beneath the wreaths. He remembered when he was a boy, tracing his fingers over the carved grooves in the chest's lid.

"This is it," he whispered. "But why is it here?"

Footsteps reverberated from the cave beneath. Someone was approaching the hole in the chapel's floor. There was no time to run. Hans pointed to a pile of goat hides in the corner. They dived underneath.

Immediately, they heard Peter hauling himself up through the hole. He shook out his cloak. "I wondered how long before you'd come again," he said sternly. "A few days ago, you tracked in dirt. Today, snow."

Hans and Angela closed their eyes tight, in hopes that he was talking to someone else. No such luck.

"I'm talking to you," he said. "Do you think I can't see the melted droplets leading to those goat hides? Come out and face me."

Angela crawled out of hiding.

"Where's your friend?"

"I don't know. I'm alone."

"No, she's not," Hans confessed. He threw off the hides and rose to his feet. "Please don't blame Angela. It was my idea to come."

"She's old enough to think for herself," Peter glowered. "This is my sanctuary. Why did you violate my trust?"

"Because it holds the secret to my past," Hans said simply. "All my life, I've been a stranger to myself. I came here to know who I am and where I'm from."

"A foolish lie. This room has nothing to do with you."

Hans pointed to the wall. "That crest has *everything* to do with me."

"Don't mock me," Peter warned.

"I'm not. When I was a baby, a man locked me in a chest and threw it into the sea. That crest was carved in the lid of the box."

The hermit rocked on his feet. "You said your father was a grave robber."

"The one who found and raised me, yes," Hans said. "Of my birth parents, sir, I know nothing."

The hermit's eyes grew wild. "It cannot be," he gasped. "Show me your right shoulder."

Hans looked to Angela.

"Do it," she said.

"And quickly," Peter urged, "before I lose my wits forever."

Hans tore off his coat and opened his shirt. Peter grabbed his arm and gazed at the birthmark perched upon his shoulder. "It's the shape of an eagle," he whispered in awe.

"I've had it since I was born."

"Of course you have. I've never forgotten." Peter draped his cloak around Hans and clutched him to his chest.

"You were at my birth?" Hans asked in bewilderment. "How? What do you know?"

"Yes, tell," Angela echoed.

Peter struggled to collect himself. "Years ago, a man sailed the sea with his infant son. He was betrayed by his brother, who'd paid the ship's captain and mate for their deaths. The traitors killed the loyal crew in their sleep and came for the man and his boy. But the man had wakened to the cries of the boatswain. He locked his baby in a chest that had once belonged to his wife and leaped with it into the waves. For hours he held firm, but a surge snatched it from

175

his grip and carried it away."

Hans could barely breathe. "What happened to the man?"

"He was discovered on a beach, wailing like a madman," Peter said. "His mind restored, he left the world to become the hermit you see before you."

Hans trembled. "Father?"

"The very same."

They threw themselves into each other's arms, and in that moment, the years of separation vanished.

31
ATTACK

ngela was overwhelmed by the reunion. Her heart swelled with happiness for Hans, but her insides choked with loneliness.

Peter saw her pain. "It's all right, child. It's hard to share joy when it awakens grief. Your parents. Yet give me a chance and I shall be your father and mother, too, till you're together with your own."

Hans and Peter opened their arms. Angela ran to them. The three embraced.

At that moment, there was a clanging of the great hall bell and the cries of hermits racing to the chapel. "Attack!

We're under attack!"

Peter threw open the door. Arrows were flying up from beyond the far ledge and raining down on the plateau. Six hermits scurried inside covering their heads with the tops of wine barrels. "There're soldiers fifty yards below the ledge."

"To the catapult," Peter commanded.

The hermits dived through the hole in the floor.

"What use is the catapult?" Angela asked. "There's nothing to aim at."

"Watch and learn," Peter said, as more hermits poured into the chapel and followed their friends down into the cave and up to the catapult beyond.

"I need a sword and shield for the fight," Hans said.

"No," Peter said. "Whatever happens, you must survive. The future of the archduchy depends on it."

"What?"

"No time to talk now." Peter grabbed the maps, bound them in two tight rolls, and slid each into a leather quiver. "These are maps of the capital, the countryside, the market square, and the palace. Keep them safe whatever you do."

Hans and Angela secured the quivers under their coats. Peter tossed them two barrel lids discarded by the hermits. "Hold these over your heads and follow me."

They raced behind Peter to the barn, arrows raining down around them. Inside, they sprinted to the stacks of wine barrels and caskets in the workshop.

Peter hoisted a large coffin above his shoulders. "This should fit the two of you."

Angela leaped back. "You mean to bury us?"

"No, to speed you to safety. Get underneath. We'll run to the right side of the ledge."

Hans and Angela followed Peter's lead. As they reached the cliff face, a boulder from the catapult sailed over their heads and disappeared into space.

Peter flipped the coffin over. "Hop in."

"I don't understand," Hans said. An arrow plunged into the ground to his right.

"Just do it!" Angela yelled. He did, Angela right behind.

"Wherever you are, fear not, for I am with you," Peter said. "I've lost you once and never shall again!" He shoved the coffin over the ledge. It sped down the slope.

"The coffin's a sled!" Angela screamed. "How do we steer it?"

"We can't," Hans screamed back as they scissored between two berry bushes. To the left, soldiers on the goat paths stared agape as they whizzed past.

Hans and Angela looked back to see a second boulder catapult high in the air. It crashed on the lip of the ledge and took three wild bounces down the rock face. On each bounce, boulders and ice shattered loose, smashing and cracking the stones and snowpack beneath them.

The slope trembled. The heavy drifts broke free from

the mountain. They tumbled earthward. It was an avalanche, carrying all before it.

Hans and Angela had been scared of the speed of their coffin-sled. Now they were scared it wasn't fast enough. The avalanche was gaining. It drowned their cries in its roar. To their left, soldiers and archers were carried away in massive balls of ice and snow. One ball bounced off a rock behind them and sailed screaming over their heads.

As the barrage overtook them, Hans threw his weight against the coffin's right side. Its back end shot left, carrying Angela's weight with it. The coffin banked on its edge and careened right, sweeping around to the far side of the mountain, out of the path of the avalanche.

But not out of danger. Now, as they hurtled to level ground, the snow disappeared. They slid at breakneck speed over grass and stone. Ahead, a sheer drop. They sailed over the edge and plummeted into the white-water rapids of a mountain river. The coffin spun like a dervish.

"Hang on!" Hans shouted.

"I am!" Angela shouted back.

"I know! To me! I mean hang on to the sides of the coffin."

The vessel barreled downstream, far from the archduke's encampment. The main river coursed into the great forest, but Hans and Angela came aground in a side stream.

Hans took off his boots and hopped into the water,

wading with the coffin to a clearing amid a stand of river reeds.

"We're alive," Angela gasped, as Hans lifted her to dry land.

"Yes, but what about Father and the others?"

"They'll be all right, Hans. I know it. Your father's a leader."

"My father." Hans lingered on the word, overwhelming and strange.

"I know you're worried," Angela said. "I would be, too. But we need to concentrate. Arnulf will be after us. We have to find food, make plans. It's what your father would want."

"My father. Peter. My father." Hans pressed his palms to his temples. Panic shot across his face. "Did the maps survive?"

Hans and Angela threw off their soaked coats and slid the maps from their quivers. Relief: The leather casings had kept them dry. Angela smoothed the map of the palace.

Hans shook his head in puzzlement. "How could Father draw that?"

"Perhaps he was the architect? One of the builders?" Angela guessed. "I only care that he drew it." She pointed at the diagram of the dungeon. "My parents are likely shackled here, in the passageway between the dungeon's torture chamber and the catacombs."

"But how do you plan to get into the palace?"

"I'll figure that out when I get there."

"When *we* get there," Hans said. "I'm coming with you."

"No. Your father wants you to live. So do I. The chances of that aren't good in the palace."

"They aren't good anywhere," Hans said. "Whatever we do, we're safer together. Friends to the end."

There was a menacing growl behind them. Hans and Angela whirled around. Staring them in the face was a large hungry bear.

ACT IV

The Circus of Dancing Bears

32

THE PANDOLINIS

"Do bears swim?" Hans whispered.

"I don't know," Angela said. "The only ones I've read about talk and keep house. I think this one's different."

The bear reared on its haunches and roared.

"To the coffin," Hans said. "Push it into the current. It'll carry us away."

They spun to the coffin. No use. A second bear was sitting in it. Angela darted to the bulrushes on the right and ran headlong into a third. The beasts bared their teeth.

A horn tooted from behind the bushes and a woman strode forward. She looked like a hollyhock, tall and erect atop a pair of green clogs. Red and green ruffles burst from her bosom and hips, while a mane of orange hair erupted from her head. She clapped her hands. "Naughty *bambini!*"

The bears looked embarrassed.

A round, mustachioed man joined the woman, followed by a dazzle of children. He wore a cape of black-and-white diamond patches over burgundy pantaloons and a yellow frock coat, topped by a red flap cap. High platform shoes sent him rocketing skyward like a balloon on stilts. The dozen children, multiple sets of twins and triplets in colorful rags, did a series of flips, somersaults, and cartwheels that climaxed in a human pyramid.

"*Ciao e buongiorno!*" the man boomed. He bowed with a flourish. "I am Signor Pandolini. May I present my wife, Signora Pandolini. Our children: Maria, Giuseppe, and the Etceteras Pandolini. And last but not least, the famous Pandolini Circus of Dancing Bears—Bruno, Balthazar, and Bianca."

The bears began to fish in the river, batting trout, graylings, and chub onto the bank, where they were promptly gutted by the Pandolini children.

"You'll dine with us?" Pandolini inquired, taming his bushy eyebrows with the dab of a forefinger.

"I'm terribly sorry, but we're in a hurry," Angela said.

Hans coughed. "We'd be delighted," he corrected her. "A meal would do us good."

"*Fantastico!*" Pandolini cheered. "While the love of my life prepares the feast, let me honor you with a tour of our circus."

Hans and Angela bundled their maps and followed Pandolini through the bushes.

"Are these people crazy?" Angela whispered to Hans.

"Probably, but they've got food."

"Who cares? Arnulf is after us."

"He has to regroup from the avalanche, first. And we have to eat. We can hardly survive on dreams."

The Pandolini home was parked on the dirt road beyond the bushes. It was a brightly painted cage on wheels with metal bars and a wooden yoke.

"The padlock on the cage door doesn't work," Pandolini said. "The bears let themselves out to do their business."

"How do you pull the wagon without horses?" Hans asked.

Pandolini wiggled his eyebrows. "Who needs horses when you have bears?"

Angela peered through the bars. "Do you have other acts?"

Pandolini nearly toppled over. "Do dogs have fleas?" He leaped into the cage and swept aside a layer of straw that covered a door in the wagon floor. Beneath was a crawl space, from which he tossed up props and costumes. "We Pandolinis breathe fire, swallow swords, and perform

186

acrobatics and magic. Not long ago, we also did *commedia* with marionettes."

"Marionettes!" Angela exclaimed.

The master showman plunged into the crawl space, his burgundy butt waving in the breeze. He emerged with a basket spilling over with tangled strings, wires, and puppet limbs. "Behold!"

Angela's face fell. "What happened to them?"

Pandolini threw his wrist to his forehead and wailed. "My *bambini* use them to fight each other. I plead with them, but do they listen?"

"No! They never listen!" Signora Pandolini brayed. She barged from the bushes, bracelets jangling, hands waving to the heavens.

"Never!" Tears dripped from the tips of Pandolini's handlebar mustache. "Last week, I blink and they toss poor Arlecchino to the bears!"

"Because you blink, Arlecchino, he misses his ear!" Signora Pandolini reached between the bars and thwacked Pandolini on the nose with a spatula. "*Idiota!*" She turned to Hans and Angela. "We eat now."

Angela carried the basket of marionettes to the campfire. "Perhaps I could untangle them."

Signora Pandolini kissed her on both cheeks. "More better, you take us to your village. Introduce us to your mayor. We will perform in your town square."

"Or in a barnyard," Pandolini added. "All we ask is food, shelter, and a few coins."

"Sadly, we're not from around here," Hans fibbed. "We're a poor brother and sister on the road to visit a distant aunt."

Pandolini pointed to the reeds. "With a coffin?"

"Yes," Angela nodded. "She's dead."

"Are there no coffin makers in her village?"

Hans glared at Angela. "They died too, I'm afraid."

Signora Pandolini arched her eyebrows. "Where are your parents? Are they not attending your auntie's funeral?"

"Heavens no," Angela improvised. "They couldn't stand her. Nobody could. Not even us. In fact, the village plans a celebration."

Pandolini burst out laughing. "*Fantastico.* Never you mind about the truth." He winked. "I guess your secret. You are on the run. We too have been on the run. Circus. The life of circus."

Pandolini motioned them to the little fire, where they feasted on bread and fish with the family. Afterward, the younger children ran off to play with the bears. The oldest, Giuseppe and Maria, stayed for a time, but as Hans and Angela spoke no Italian, they soon grew bored and wandered off as well.

Signor and Signora Pandolini regaled Hans and Angela with tales of the road:

"In Anatolia, Bianca did a pirouette on the high wire

for the sultan," Pandolini enthused, stripping a fillet of fish with his teeth and tossing the head into the pot of guts his wife was boiling for a soup.

"And in Bohemia," Signora Pandolini said as she stirred the broth, "the emperor fainted when the children juggled axes."

"While swinging by their toes on a trapeze," Pandolini added.

Angela's fingers flew as fast as the Pandolinis' tongues. By the time the showman told of the time he turned a Hapsburg prince into a parrot, she'd untangled the marionettes and had the puppet Scapino dancing on a boulder.

Pandolini clapped his hands to his cheeks. "You've saved them! *Grazie*."

"I've always dreamed of playing the great courts of Europe," Angela declaimed in the voice of the string man.

Signor Pandolini tossed his cap in the air. "Bravo! Bravissimo!"

Two of the children ran up from the water, pointing and babbling. The Pandolinis jumped to their feet. Signora Pandolini put her hand to her throat. *"Madre de Dio!"*

"What is it?" Hans asked.

"Soldiers," Pandolini said. "They scout the riverbank."

Hans and Angela turned to run.

"Stay where you are!" Pandolini exclaimed with a sweep of his cape.

189

"But it's us they're after," Hans said.

"Never fear. We shall hide you where even the fox dares not go."

"No," Angela protested. "We won't put your family in danger."

"What kind of family abandons children?" Signora Pandolini demanded.

In a flash, they spirited Hans and Angela into the crawl space of the circus wagon. Pandolini stuffed costumes after them and covered the floor doors with straw, while his wife and children put the bears in the cage above them.

A dozen soldiers burst through the reeds, as Pandolini snapped the broken padlock in place. The soldiers aimed their muskets at the Pandolinis' heads.

"*Ciao e buongiorno!*" The showman beamed. "I am Signor Pandolini. May I present my wife, Signora Pandolini. Our children, Maria, Giuseppe, and the Etceteras Pandolini! Last but not least, our Circus of Dancing Bears."

The captain eyed Pandolini with suspicion. "We're looking for two young vagabonds."

"*Vagabondi!*" Signora Pandolini gathered her children close.

"They were last seen fleeing down a mountain in a coffin," the captain said. "A coffin like the one in the reeds by your campsite."

"It was here when we arrived," Pandolini said. "Perhaps

they fell in the water and drowned?"

"Or perhaps they hide among you," the captain replied. "Show us your brats. If any boy is found with the mark of an eagle on his shoulder or any girl with golden locks, they shall die at once, and the rest of you after."

The soldiers examined the Pandolini children. Their hair was as dark as a raven; their skin as clear as olive oil. The captain glanced at the bear cage. "Do these monsters really dance?"

"Do witches fly on broomsticks?" Pandolini snapped his fingers. "Bruno! Balthazar! Bianca!" The bears rose on their hind legs and performed a bored minuet.

"What other acts do you have?"

"We juggle, tumble, and swallow swords," Pandolini said proudly. "We also perform with marionettes!"

"Hmm. The archduke loves puppets," the captain said. "Within days, he'll be at the palace, in need of amusement. Entertain him and you shall be rewarded."

The Pandolinis exchanged glances.

"We are honored," Pandolini said. "Yet another time, perhaps. At the moment, we're headed to Poland."

The soldiers cocked their muskets.

"At the moment," the captain said, "you're headed to the palace."

33

TO THE PALACE

*T*he captain placed the circus under the guard of three soldiers and left with the rest of his men to hunt for Hans and Angela downstream. The soldiers harnessed the bears, put the Pandolinis in the cage, and steered the wagon around the great forest, traveling west till the tree line made a grand diagonal south to the capital.

On the first night, while the soldiers erected their tent, Maria, Giuseppe, and the Etceteras swung from the cage bars. Under cover of movement and shadow, Hans and Angela emerged from the crawl space in colorful costume rags; Signora Pandolini's jet-black fortune-teller's wig was secured over Angela's blond curls.

"*Assomigliate a noi*," Giuseppe said excitedly.

"Our son says you look just like him and the others." Pandolini smiled.

Maria batted her eyes at Hans. "*Sei molto bello.*"

Hans flushed. "Thank you, I think?"

Angela gave Maria the evil eye—and Hans an elbow in the ribs.

"It's terrible for you to be trapped by your enemy," Pandolini said.

"Not at all," Angela replied. "We're on a quest to rescue my parents from the archduke's palace. How better to get inside than disguised as entertainers?"

"Angela's right," Hans agreed. "The terrible thing is how we endanger your family. We shouldn't have let you hide us."

Signora Pandolini flicked her hand. "Shush. Who knows the future? Do the best you can and never regret a kindness. To live a coward is not to live at all."

"Besides," Pandolini said, "you won't be discovered. People see what they expect: Expect to see kerchiefs turn into doves, and you shall. Expect to see monsters in shadows, there they'll be. Expect a simple band of children, that's all that will appear." He winked. "Who'd dream that those with a price on their head would break into a bear cage guarded by the archduke's troops?"

◆　◆　◆

The next day, as the circus cage lumbered to the palace, the Pandolini children taught their guests a little Italian. Soon, Hans and Angela knew how to say *please* and *thank you*, the parts of the face, and the lyrics to six folk songs. The soldiers paid no heed, too worried about warlock-monsters lurking in the trees.

Midday, the Pandolinis had a siesta, and Hans and Angela memorized their maps. To shield them from view, they put them at the bottom of a nest of straw and lay on either side. "The memorial pillar to Archduke Fredrick has its foundations in the catacombs," Hans observed.

Angela nodded. "It's so massive it would have to. Otherwise it would've collapsed the excavation under it."

Hans ran a finger along the underground lagoon at the far end of the dungeon and the red markings on the upper palace floors. He counted the rooms in each corridor. "Why do you think Father said the archduchy's future depends on me?"

"Hermits always say strange things," Angela shrugged. "At least in books," she quickly corrected. "There's nothing strange about your father. Peter is wonderful. He loves you, too, unlike that old grave robber."

"Don't be mean about my other papa," Hans said. "He raised me as well as he could."

"To rob graves."

A guard rattled the bars. "What's going on?"

Angela rolled over on the maps. "*Buongiorno,*" she chirped.

Hans waved. "*Prego e grazie.*"

The guard peered through the bars. "What's that supposed to mean?"

Pandolini roused. "It means my children are *idioti!*"

Angela agreed, spouting the first Italian folk lyric she could remember.

"*Naso, occhi, bocca,*" Hans nodded, naming off parts of the face.

Pandolini pretended to smack Hans on the side of the head.

"Hit him again," the guard laughed. Pandolini obliged. "Circus ragamuffins," the guard sneered, and returned to his comrades.

Pandolini patted Hans and Angela warmly. "*Piccoli pappagalli.*" He smiled. "You'll soon be warbling like Venetians."

The third day passed as the second, Hans and Angela learning Italian and memorizing maps. But at dusk, all study ceased; they'd reached the edge of the capital.

Through fingers of fog, Hans and Angela saw the forest on their left. On their right, clapboard houses clustered on a web of dirt roads that skirted a steep, rocky hill. A stone tower rose from its peak; howls echoed through its small, barred windows.

"What is that place?" Pandolini asked.

"The asylum," a soldier said.

A breeze stirred the dank air with the reek of the grave. Signora Pandolini fanned herself with a tarot card.

"The dumping grounds," said another guard, his nose pressed into his arm. "Doctors dissect the madmen when they die, then toss them on the dung heaps."

They entered the city. Angela remembered the sooty oil lamps along the ghostly maze of narrow streets and, now, the grand public square with its magnificent buildings. "The cathedral," she murmured to Hans. "Between it and the palace, the memorial pillar with the marble coffins for Fredrick, his wife, and infant son."

Hans peered up at the gargoyled spires, turrets, and parapets of the palace. "It's exactly as Father drew it," he whispered. Angela nodded.

The wagon stopped. The guards lined up their prisoners. The palace doors swung wide. Inside, the vaulted entry hall was alive with servants in dark velvet livery. The Spoon emerged, conferred with the guards, and strode to Pandolini. "I am the chief steward," he announced with a click of his heels. "His Royal Highness is secluded with the lord high chancellor. You will entertain them tomorrow night."

"*Ciao e buonasera!*" Pandolini beamed. At times like this it was best to appear simple.

The Spoon ordered the bear cage to the courtyard next to

the laundry room and directed the company to sleep by the washtubs. Angela feared he'd recognize her, but Pandolini was right: the Spoon expected no more than urchins in colorful rags, and that's all he saw.

The Pandolinis kissed their children, cuddled in a heap around them. *"Buona notte,"* they whispered to Hans and Angela. In minutes, they were snoring a duet.

Angela nudged Hans. "Now's our chance. Do you remember the route from the laundry to the dungeon?"

"Of course. The map showed a hall from here to the kitchen and storage areas. Beyond is the circular ramp that'll take us down into hell."

"That's right," Angela said. "Let's go."

THE SECRET PASSAGEWAY

*H*ans and Angela crept out of the darkened laundry. They pressed themselves against the wall of the corridor and slid to the kitchen entrance.

Three vats, six spits, an enormous stove, and a stack of firewood ran down one side of the kitchen. An oak counter and cupboards, interrupted by a spiral staircase, ran down the other. At the far end, a lamp lit the entrance to the storage areas. An elderly cook rocked on a stool beside it, faced away toward a slop trough, peeling potatoes.

"How do we get past her?" Angela whispered.

Hans nodded to the spiral staircase. "We can go up to

the banquet hall, cross over, and take stairs down on the other side."

"Good plan."

They edged silently through the kitchen. As they reached the staircase, the cook loosed a great sneeze. She turned around, rubbing her eyes.

Hans and Angela ran up the stairs. Past the first spiral, the light dimmed. Past the second it disappeared. They touched the outer wall and slowly made their way to a landing. There was a short walkway to a wall of velvet curtains. Light shone through the slit where they'd been pulled together.

"This is it," Angela whispered. "The banquet hall's beyond."

Hans and Angela peered through the draperies. A stern-faced woman was adjusting chairs. "That's the housekeeper who poured me a bath," Angela gasped. "I'll bet she poured the milk that drowned Georgina, too."

Hans frowned. "With her here, we'll have to cross above."

The housekeeper looked at the curtains. "Who's there?" She marched toward them. "I said, who's there?"

Hans and Angela ran back to the spiral staircase and scrambled up into the dark, the housekeeper in pursuit. Eight spirals later they burst into a torchlit corridor. They turned left and ran past a series of doors flanked by suits of armor. As the housekeeper entered the hall, they dived between sets of decorative chain mail coats and leggings.

There was a strange silence, save for the housekeeper's labored breathing. "It's you, isn't it, Georgina? You've come back," she said at last. Her voice was full of fear and regret. "Or is it you, Isabella? Or you, Clara? Or maybe it's all of you I hear, walking these halls, haunting these stairs and parapets. Leave me alone. Please. It wasn't my doing." Her whimpers disappeared down the staircase.

Angela shivered. "Hans, I've been in this hallway. It's where Arnulf locked me when I was first here. But the spirals have spun me around so much I'm not sure which way we're facing. We could be crossing the banquet hall or going in the opposite direction."

Hans paused. "With the housekeeper down those stairs, we can't go back the way we came. We can't stay here, either. Anyone could come around a corner and see us." He wet his lips. "According to the map, there's a hidden passageway behind the rooms. But how do we find it?"

Angela thought of the nighttime visit of the last archduchess. "The paintings! The entrances are behind the paintings!" She opened the door to a pitch-black room. "Grab a torch."

Hans took a torch from a sconce in the corridor and

followed Angela into the room. On one wall there was a depiction of the devil swallowing lost souls. Angela ran her hands behind the frame. She felt a catch and pressed it. Nothing happened. After a flurry of fingers, she found a second catch. She pressed them both. The painting swung open.

Angela peered through the holes in the devil's eyes. "This is how Arnulf spies on his guests."

Hans wasn't listening. He was headed back to the corridor.

"What are you doing?"

"Returning this torch. If it's missing, it'll draw attention. Besides, its light would shine through the peepholes and give us away."

"How will we keep from getting lost?" Angela panicked.

"We'll count our steps. If we're lucky, we'll find stairs leading down to the storage area. If not, we'll retrace our steps."

In a moment, he returned and shut the door. Angela found his hand in the dark, drew him into the secret passageway, and closed the painting. They inched forward, hands held high to protect their heads from support beams.

After two hundred steps, the corridor forked in two. They turned left. A few steps more and Hans stubbed his toe. "We've reached stairs," he said, "but they go up not down."

Ahead, two dots of light pierced the inky black: peep-holes. The sickly sweet smell of camphor, mandrake, and rotting flesh drifted through the holes. Hans and Angela heard a familiar voice on the other side.

"Lord High Chancellor," Arnulf said. "I need council from the land of the dead."

THE THREE PROPHECIES

Hans and Angela crept up to the peepholes, hearts pounding.

A fog of incense billowed from five upturned skulls hanging from the ceiling. Alcoves filled with animal entrails surrounded a sacrificial stone.

Archduke Arnulf, draped in a hooded robe, knelt in a hexagon outlined with candles. The Necromancer stood behind him, stroking a goat head. His eye sockets were fitted with a pair of glass palace doorknobs. They sparkled in the candlelight—two glittering balls of madness.

Hans and Angela looked on in horror.

"What would you know from the land of the dead?" the

Necromancer asked in a singsong voice.

The vein at Arnulf's temple throbbed. "Shall I ever be rid of the boy and the girl?"

"Yes, to be sure."

"But they've escaped again."

"Not for long." The Necromancer nuzzled the goat head. "The hermitage is destroyed. There's nowhere for them to hide. Soon the great forest will have been combed as thoroughly as a coronation wig—and they shall be ours."

"The girl's parents will pay," Arnulf muttered. "I thought they'd be destroyed when I gave them a dinner tray bearing a roasted heart and their daughter's jewels. Instead, they mocked me: 'If our Angela were truly dead, you'd have presented us with her head.'"

"They'll fall in time, Excellency. None can long withstand the lunatic asylum."

Angela gripped Hans' hand: Her parents weren't in the palace after all; they were caged with madmen in the terrible stone tower at the city's edge.

"Then there's the boy," Arnulf said. "The grave robber's apprentice. He should have died with his father."

"But Excellency, the grave robber's alive in the dungeon."

Hans' ears perked up.

"No, I don't mean the grave robber," Arnulf exclaimed. "I mean the father that the boy was born to: my elder brother, Archduke Fredrick."

Hans nearly choked. *My father—Peter the Hermit—is Archduke Fredrick?*

The Necromancer scratched his chin with a goat horn. "The world thinks Fredrick and his son were killed by pirates."

"A fetching tale," Arnulf said, "but surely you know the truth from wandering my dreams."

"Indeed I do," the Necromancer lied.

Arnulf rocked on his knees, his mind bedeviled. "I bribed the ship's captain and mate to slay Fredrick and his baby at sea. As planned, when the ship returned, they reported a deadly attack by pirates. I executed them on the spot to bury the truth forever."

"Then what have you to fear?" the Necromancer soothed.

"The boy. He's heir to the throne."

"Why? Even if he knew his history, who'd believe a grave robber's apprentice? The past is a graveyard of secrets, where truth lies buried in legend."

"Still, sleep escapes me." Arnulf beat his head on the floor. "I need the spirits' counsel: Need I fear the boy?"

The Necromancer cradled the goat head and droned incantations as he waltzed around the room, the glass doorknobs in his sockets spinning shards of light. He stopped in front of Arnulf and placed a speck of woodland fungus on the archduke's tongue.

Arnulf was overcome by visions. He rolled between the candles. "I see a legion of my enemies! A swarm of rats running off with my crown."

"Take heart." The Necromancer took entrails from an alcove and slopped them on the floor. He ran his fingers over the intestines. "Hear the prophecy of the spirits: You shall reign till the great forest marches on the capital!"

"A forest march?" Arnulf convulsed in joy. "Impossible! I see my enemies quake before me."

The Necromancer threw the guts a second time. He felt the liver and spleen. "A second time, the spirits prophesy: You shall reign till an eagle rises from stone."

"An eagle rise from stone? Again, impossible. My enemies flee."

The Necromancer sniffed the kidneys. "A third and final time, the spirits prophesy: You shall reign till your severed hands sail over a sea of bones."

Arnulf howled in triumph. "This is the best of all!" He patted the golden reliquary hanging from his neck. "My severed hands shall never move again. Nor have I ever seen a sea of bones, nor shall ever sail upon one."

The Necromancer smiled. "Sleep well, Excellency. Tomorrow messengers shall spread these prophecies about the land. None will dare challenge the word of the spirit world."

Arnulf swept his greasy locks from his forehead. "Thank you, O wise Lord High Chancellor. You shall have treasure anon." He strode from the room.

The Necromancer placed the guts and goat head on the sacrificial stone and went to follow. Hans and Angela gaped at each other in the dark.

"Archduke Fredrick is your father," Angela whispered in awe. "Hans, you're a prince—the heir to the throne. No wonder the archduchy's future rests in you."

"Forget about me," Hans said. "What about your parents?"

"What about them indeed?" came a voice as dead as leaves in winter.

Hans and Angela turned to the peepholes. Two glittering doorknobs peered at them from the other side.

"I missed your scents in the incense," the Necromancer cooed. "Did you miss mine?"

Hans and Angela screamed. They tripped down the stairs and stumbled to the turn, the Necromancer's laugh echoing after them. "You'll never escape these walls, my pretties. You're trapped!"

Hans and Angela darted back to the room where they'd entered the passage. In seconds, they were out the door and racing to the spiral staircase. They zipped down—holding their breath by the banquet hall—and kept on going, down, down, down to the kitchen—where they ran straight into the housekeeper.

The housekeeper seized each by an arm. "What are you monkeys up to?"

"Looking for a chamber pot," Angela babbled.

"A likely story," the housekeeper sniffed. "You're circus thieves out to loot the palace. I'm calling the guards."

"No, please," Hans said. "We heard a girl crying. We followed the sound up the stairs."

The housekeeper's eyes went big as pies. "A girl? Did you see her?"

"Yes." Angela played along. "She was covered in worms, dripping milk. Her name is Georgina."

The housekeeper fell back against the woodpile. "*Aaa!* You didn't see me! I didn't see you. Tonight didn't happen! Please!" She flew from the kitchen and into the storage area, where she hid in a barrel of chestnuts.

Hans and Angela hurried to the laundry room, roused the Pandolinis, and told them their news.

"The Necromancer could be here at any moment," Hans said. "He knows our scent. We're done for!"

"We are never done for. We are Pandolinis," the showman exclaimed.

Signora Pandolini reached into her nibble bag and produced a dozen bulbs of garlic. "Rub cloves on your skin and chew the rest. Then let the devil try to sniff you out!"

◆ ◆ ◆

Hans and Angela lay awake all night, but the Necromancer never came. That meant only one thing. He was waiting to strike. But when?

36

THE PANDOLINI TRANSFORMATORIUM

*S*hortly after dawn, town criers trumpeted the Necromancer's prophecies. Waves of gossip roiled Market Square: Archduke Arnulf was destined to reign forever; resistance was futile.

Inside the palace, soldiers escorted Hans, Angela, and the Pandolinis to the banquet hall to rehearse the evening's entertainment. A platform had been erected on a dozen trestles opposite the archduke's massive mahogany table. The bear cage had been rolled up the rear circular ramp and braced beside the stage.

The company warmed up. Pandolini performed a series of hums, tongue rolls, and facial contortions; his wife rigged his magic coat with cards, scarves, and collapsible props; Maria, Giuseppe, and the Etceteras did stretching exercises; Hans and Angela laid out the marionettes; and Bruno, Balthazar, and Bianca groomed each other's ears.

Without warning, there was a fanfare of trumpets and Arnulf and the Necromancer were carried into the hall on golden litters. The company dropped to the floor. Arnulf clapped his iron hands. The boards shook on their trestles. "Rise."

Signor Pandolini bowed low. "*Ciao e buongiorno!*" he said with a sunny smile. "I am Signor Pandolini! May I present—"

"No," Arnulf interrupted coldly. "Unless you mean to present the two new additions to your troupe: a grave robber's apprentice and a countess."

Hans, Angela, and the Pandolinis looked at each other and bolted for the doors. Guards leaped into position, swords drawn. The company jumped back.

"There's no escape," Arnulf advised calmly. "Soldiers are double-ranked behind the curtains that circle this room, and an entire garrison is stationed at both front and rear entrances to the palace. Should you dream of leaping from windows or turrets, know that the windows are barred and the lowest turret is over one hundred feet above hard cobblestones."

Hans stepped forward. "I'm the one you're after. These

good people knew nothing of my past. Whatever you do to me, spare them."

"And your little friend, too?" the Necromancer asked slyly.

"No," Angela said, stepping to Hans' side. "Do with me what you will as well, but release my parents."

"It's rather early in the day for pretty speeches," Arnulf replied. "And rather late to be giving orders."

Signor and Signora Pandolini knelt before the archduke. "Our children. Spare our children."

"That's what they all say," Arnulf yawned. He stroked the reliquary box on the chain around his neck. "Cheer up. I'd intended to kill you all before breakfast, but since I love the circus, I'm letting you live till after the performance. How fitting—the final curtain will be your own."

Pandolini leaped to his feet. "O Mightiest of the Mighty, if we're to die, let our final act be the Pandolini Transformatorium!"

"What, pray, is the Pandolini Transformatorium?"

"Only the greatest circus act the world has ever seen!" Pandolini declaimed. "And yet . . ." He paused dramatically. "I must deny you."

"Who are you to deny me?"

"Alas, Your Highness, the Transformatorium must be constructed. We lack both tools and materials."

"What do you need?"

"Two dozen wooden slats, a bolt of cheesecloth, a hammer, a saw, and nails."

Arnulf laughed. "That's nothing."

"Please, Your Highness, refuse him," Signora Pandolini pleaded. "Let us die in peace. Spare us the terror of the Transformatorium!"

Arnulf cocked an eyebrow. "I delight in terror." He turned to a soldier. "Bring the materials forthwith." He snapped his fingers. The clang reverberated around the vaulted ceiling. Attendants sprang to the litters and conveyed the archduke and the Necromancer from the hall.

Pandolini winked at Hans and Angela. "Remember we said we once turned a Hapsburg prince into a parrot? The Tranformatorium did the trick. Tonight, it will do one better. At my signal, our entire circus will disappear!"

37
A NIGHT AT THE CIRCUS

All day, the banquet hall was a hive of activity. The Etceteras draped fabric around the bottom of the stage, hung circus banners at the back and sides, and decorated the adjoining bear cage with bunting; Hans and Giuseppe hammered and sawed behind screens; and Angela and Maria made costumes and marionettes. Whenever soldiers came up to inspect, Signor and Signora Pandolini wailed prayers more passionate than opera and invited them to dance with Bianca.

At last it was time for the banquet. The company clustered under a row of lamps at the foot of the trestle stage, while Arnulf and the Necromancer feasted opposite by torchlight at the mahogany table. Between them, soldiers squatted on low stools in a swath of gloom.

Arnulf rose. The room stilled. "As all the land knows, last night the spirit world blessed me with three prophecies: I shall reign till the great forest marches on the capital; till an eagle rises from stone; and till these dead hands sail over a sea of bones!" He waved the reliquary box above his head in triumph.

"Long live Arnulf, Archduke of Waldland!" his soldiers cheered.

"To celebrate, I give you the Pandolini Circus!" Arnulf exulted. "Proceed, mountebanks."

The company took their places. The shutters on the lamps downstage were opened wide. Signor Pandolini trod the boards, his cheeks painted red, his eyelids indigo, his mustache waxed and bristling.

"*Ciao e buonasera.* I am Signor Pandolini, and this is the Pandolini Circus of Dancing Bears." (Theatrical "Oohs" from the Pandolinis in the wings.) "Tonight, you will see jugglers and acrobats." (Theatrical "Aahs" from the backstage Pandolinis.) "Dancing bears." (Theatrical "Grrs" from Bruno, Balthazar, and Bianca.) "Last, but not least, you will thrill to the magical Pandolini Transformatorium!" (Boisterous "Huzzahs" from the soldiers.)

"First—*acrobati*! Maria, Giuseppe, and the Etceteras!" The children tumbled onstage. They juggled torches and

215

tambourines, did cartwheels and backflips, and contorted themselves like pretzels. For their climax, they leaped on each other's shoulders and formed three columns; the moppets on top somersaulted from one to the other. The soldiers hollered themselves hoarse.

Pandolini flourished his cape. "Now, *amici*, the dancing bears!" The children scampered offstage as Bruno, Balthazar, and Bianca roused from their lethargy. They stood on their hind paws and performed a series of pavanes, pirouettes, and promenades, while Signora Pandolini, wearing a hat of ostrich plumes and glass beads, played ballroom music on a fiddle.

Next, Pandolini swallowed a dagger, a side sword, and a rapier. Signora Pandolini levitated a rope from a bucket. And then—

Archduke Arnulf clapped his iron hands. "Enough. We would see the Transformatorium."

"Have mercy!" Pandolini begged. "It is the final act before we die. Perhaps a card trick?"

The archduke drummed his fingers on the table. The cutlery rattled. "No."

Pandolini motioned his family downstage, as Hans and Angela placed the troupe's collapsible puppet theater upstage behind them.

Pandolini's eyes bugged wide. "Many times I have called my children blockheads. Tonight, by means of the Pandolini

Transformatorium, I shall transform them into that very thing: Blocks of wood. Marionettes."

Hans and Angela put a shuttered lantern on either side of the puppet theater; Signora Pandolini and her brood placed a wall of cheesecloth screens between the theater and the showman.

"Maria! Giuseppe!" Pandolini called. Signora Pandolini and Hans opened the shutters of the upstage lanterns. As the area flooded with light, the cheesecloth seemed to disappear; Maria and Giuseppe were seen in red jerkins covered in blue ribbons.

"Hello, Papà," they said in unison.

Pandolini waved a wand. "Become the blockheads you were meant to be!" The lanterns went dark; the screens became opaque. He waved the wand again. The light returned; the screens were transparent. But instead of Maria and Giuseppe, two marionettes in red jerkins with blue ribbons danced on the puppet proscenium.

Angela pulled their strings and impersonated their pitiful voices. "Papà!" cried puppet Maria. "Papà!" cried puppet Giuseppe. The audience slapped its thighs and hooted.

"Now, the rest of you rapscallions! Show yourselves!" Pandolini cried. The Etceteras ran onstage behind the transparent screens.

"Begone!" Pandolini cried with a wave of his wand.

The lights dimmed; the children vanished. A wave of the wand, and the lights returned. The children had been replaced by rows of marionettes that jumped and cavorted as Angela jiggled a grid of rods, and shrieked a babble of squeals. Even greater laughter and applause shook the hall.

"May the newest members of my troupe present themselves," Pandolini commanded.

Angela stepped from behind the puppet theater in a swashbuckler's costume. She joined Hans at center stage behind the gauze.

"Worse than blockheads, you shall become kindling to light the archduke's fires!" Pandolini declaimed. He scurried to the lamp abandoned by Hans. "Begone!" He and Signora Pandolini darkened the lamps. At once, the screens became opaque.

The soldiers stared at the wall of cheesecloth. A pause became a silence.

"Why the delay?" Arnulf called to Pandolini. "Show us their puppet selves."

"*Un momento!*" Pandolini called from behind the screens. More silence. The soldiers began to grumble.

"Finish the trick!" Arnulf warned.

"*Un momento. Un momento.*"

The grumbling grew. The archduke rose. "Signor Pandolini!"

"*Sì. Un momento.*" The voice was distant, muffled.

Arnulf's pupils twitched. "Guards!"

Soldiers stormed the platform and ripped away the gauze screens.

To Arnulf's horror—the entire circus troupe had vanished!

"What's going on?" he cried.

The soldiers smashed the puppet theater. They tore down the banners and threw open the curtains around the hall. There was no one there but the archduke's troops, ringing the walls and cramming the staircases.

"Where are they?" Arnulf screamed.

The Necromancer polished his doorknobs. "They haven't gone up, and they haven't gone out. That can mean only one thing."

"What?" Arnulf shrieked.

"They've gone down."

"*Down?*" Arnulf exploded. He threw over the dining table, strode to the stage, and yanked away the fabric that hung from the trestles. There, under the platform, he saw Signora Pandolini desperately trying to squash her husband's rump through a hole in the floorboards.

"They've sawed an exit beneath the stage!" Arnulf raged. "They've dropped into a secret passageway! They're scurrying through my palace like rats!"

A soldier grabbed Signora Pandolini by the elbows. Two

more seized Signor Pandolini by the legs and tried to pry him from the hole.

"The children are still trapped, Excellency," the Necromancer soothed. "There's a garrison at both front and rear gates, the windows are barred, and a leap from the turrets is death. Besides, the spirits have decreed that you shall reign till the great forest marches on the capital; till an eagle rises from stone; and till your severed hands sail over a sea of bones."

"Indeed. I've nothing to fear," Arnulf murmured, an oily sweat dripping from his chin. He turned to a dozen of his soldiers. "Take the mountebanks to the dungeon. If they fail to reveal the children's plans, toss them in the bear cage with their beasts and starve the monsters till they feed upon their masters." He turned to the rest. "Block every corridor while the chancellor and I pop down the rabbit hole. We'll find them as easily as eggs on an Easter hunt."

38

ESCAPE OF THE BAMBINI

Angela raced the Pandolini children along secret passageways and stairs to the fifth floor. The dark held no terror. The previous night had taught her how to measure distance, and the children could juggle axes blindfolded. Angela thought of Hans, off on a perilous mission of his own, and of the bravery of Signor and Signora Pandolini. Their plan to use the showman's bottom to block Arnulf's pursuit had bought her precious time.

Angela scrambled out of a painting in the art gallery, a room filled with portraits and tapestries of the arch-duke's wives: Georgina in a bathtub, Isabella leaning over a parapet, and the last archduchess tumbling toward a set of doors with bronze knobs like the archduke's hands.

"*Rapidamente!*" she called to the children. They dashed after her to the archway at the end of the gallery and up the stairs beyond. At the top was a door. Angela undid the bolts and threw it open. True to the map, they'd arrived on the roof of the east turret, well out of sight of the palace entrances.

The stone railing was ringed with gargoyles. Angela leaned over. The cobblestones below looked as far away as home.

The Pandolini children whipped magician's scarves from their sleeves and knotted the ends together. Six feet of scarves from each of the twelve meant seventy-two feet of silk rope, far short of what was needed.

Giuseppe saw the fear in Angela's eyes and winked. He tied one end of the silk rope around a winged gargoyle. Then he threw the rest of the rope over the turret, made a loop for his arm, and slid down its length. He clung to the bottom while the largest of his brothers slid down after him. They hooked their legs together, Giuseppe's brother now hanging below him, head to the cobblestones.

The next in height followed, locking arms with Giuseppe's brother; and then the next, locking legs with the third to make a chain of four. So it went by height and strength, the Pandolini children linking arms and legs, each body bringing the chain closer to the ground. The last on the chain swayed near the pavement.

It was Angela's turn. There was no time to lose. Giuseppe could barely hang on—and there were soldiers' shouts coming from the gallery.

Angela hopped over the turret roof and slipped down the rope, six brothers, and several of the sisters. Approaching the ground, she felt the little locked limbs begin to fail. She jumped, scraping her hands on the cobblestones.

No matter. She hopped to her feet and stood beneath the chain of children. "*Ora*," she cried to the tiniest Pandolini, who unlocked her legs and fell into Angela's arms. The second and third followed suit. Angela linked arms with the trio and caught the fourth and fifth. Now the five Pandolinis on the ground pressed their backs to the palace wall and climbed on each other's shoulders, the strongest on the bottom.

The human pillar rose higher than the lowest child left dangling. The girl unlocked her legs and slid down her siblings to the ground. A brother followed. The pillar regrouped, with the stronger new arrivals at the base. Three more of the danglers slid down.

There was a quick regroup as Arnulf and his soldiers poured onto the turret roof. No sooner had Giuseppe's last brother let go of his legs and shimmied away than Arnulf raised his sword. He severed the rope as Giuseppe, too, slid down his siblings to safety.

Arnulf watched the pillar of children melt from top to bottom. Enraged, he smashed a gargoyle with his fist. Chunks of stone crashed to the cobblestones, but all Arnulf heard was the sound of children's laughter disappearing into the mist.

39
INTO THE DUNGEON

*M*eanwhile, Hans was feeling every lurch and rumble as soldiers rolled the bear cage down the circular ramp from the banquet hall to the dungeon. With everyone focused on the Transformatorium, he'd slipped from the wings to the back of the bear cage. There, under cover of darkness and bunting, he'd fiddled the prop lock and petted his way into the wagon's crawl space.

Hans wished he were with Angela, but he had a role to play. Signor and Signora Pandolini had guessed that Arnulf would send them and their bears to the dungeon; Hans had volunteered to hide in the crawl space and rescue them. He had someone else to save as well: his other papa, Knobbe.

Now, as the cage rattled into the fetid underworld, Hans seized his purpose: to forge from the terrible things he'd endured a life heroic. He'd save his friends and his papa. If he lived, he'd save the archduchy, too, and restore his father, Peter the Hermit—Archduke Fredrick—to the throne.

The cage ground to a halt. Through a crack in the side-boards, Hans saw a gloomy cavern lit by a few torches and a fire pit. The flames cast light and shadow over rock walls hung with frightening instruments. Moans drifted in from an archway on the right, while the sound of water dripping into a vast pool echoed out of the dark at the far end of the cavern.

Hans pictured the map of the dungeon. It showed a tor-ture chamber connected to the cathedral by a prison and catacombs running under Market Square, and to an outside bay by a vast underground lagoon. Surely the moans were coming from a prisoner in the city of bones; the dripping water, from the lagoon—the waterway to freedom.

Three hellish figures entered through the archway. The first was a brawny man with a whip. He wore an execution-er's hood and a chain mail tunic that hung over black leather trousers and boots. Two monstrous twins lurched behind him. Pale as chalk, with tiny heads and bloodshot eyes, they giggled and yelped through snaggles of rotten teeth.

The man's voice reverberated through the charnel house. "Welcome," he said to the Pandolinis. "I am the archduke's executioner and dungeon master. These are my assistants, twins from the rankest cells of the asylum."

"G'day, g'day," the twins cackled.

"*Ciao e buonasera*," Pandolini said nervously.

"Leave us," the dungeon master said to the troops. They saluted and marched up the ramp out of the cavern. He turned to his assistants and cracked his whip. "Take our visitors to the rack."

The twins grabbed the Pandolinis and dragged them to the stretching table. "Stuffing, stuffing," they giggled as they poked the showman's belly. "Pretty dolly," they gurgled at his wife. The dungeon master attached leather bindings to the Pandolinis' wrists and ankles, and fastened these to the rack's pulleys, which ran to the rafters above.

Hans had seen enough. He grabbed the bear pole in the crawl space and pushed against the door in the wagon's floor. To his horror, it wouldn't budge.

"So, my friends," the dungeon master said, "tell me your children's plans. Speak, or I'll crank the great wheel and tear you apart." The twins clapped their hands with glee.

The Pandolinis glanced at the bear cage and saw at once why Hans hadn't sprung to their rescue. Balthazar was sitting on the door to the crawl space.

Pandolini thought fast. "They didn't tell us their plans," he said. "For that, you must ask—BRUNO! BALTHAZAR! AND BIANCA!"

227

"Who are Bruno, Balthazar, and Bianca?" the dungeon master thundered.

Signora Pandolini took her cue. "Who are BRUNO? BALTHAZAR? AND BIANCA?"

"BRUNO, BALTHAZAR, and BIANCA," the Pandolinis bellowed together, "are the most terrifying creatures in all the archduchy."

"More terrifying than me?" the dungeon master scoffed.

"See for yourself," Pandolini grinned. "They're right behind you."

And indeed they were. Roused by their masters' cries, the bears had flipped the prop padlock from the cage and lumbered out to do battle. Balthazar's giant claws came down on the dungeon master's shoulder.

The dungeon master whirled around and stared straight into Balthazar's teeth. He screamed. Balthazar swiped him with the back of his paw. The dungeon master flew across the room and dropped senseless to the ground. Bruno and Bianca growled at his assistants. They fainted.

Hans roared up, wielding the bear pole. "Sorry I'm late."

"Never mind," Pandolini said, "just get us out of these straps."

Hans quickly freed the Pandolinis and got the dungeon master's keys. "Let's lock these villains out of sight."

"No need to lift a finger," Pandolini said. He barked a command in Italian.

The bears each grabbed a varlet by a leg and dragged them through the archway into the prison corridor. Skeletons hung from manacles on the walls. Some had been dismantled by rats and littered the hallway with their bones.

Hans thought of birdsongs and open skies. "An executioner's disguise may be useful," he said. He stripped off the dungeon master's uniform and shackled the rogue to the wall in his underwear. He trussed the twins on either side. "Stay here," he told the Pandolinis. "I'm off to find my papa, Knobbe."

Hans moved swiftly down the lamp-lit corridor. By now, he imagined Angela and the Pandolini children would be escaping from the turret. Once Arnulf found out they were gone, he'd be raging to the dungeon to take his revenge on their parents.

"Papa?" he called down dark side passageways. Was he too late? Was Knobbe already dead?

Ahead, the corridor opened onto the catacombs, a labyrinth of floor-to-ceiling shelves stacked with the bones of martyrs and soldiers from centuries past.

"Please, Papa," Hans cried. "Let me know you're alive."

There was a moan from a passageway to his left. Through the gloom, he saw Knobbe's lumpen body hanging from the wall. "Papa?" Hans ran to him.

The grave robber groaned. "Are you a spirit come to haunt me?"

"No, Papa, no."

Knobbe's eyes filled with tears. "There once was a boy who called me Papa. A boy who loved me. A boy I abused. That boy is lost to me forever."

"No, Papa, he's not. I'm here."

"Pray, do not mock me," Knobbe wept.

"Never, upon my soul." Hans unshackled him from the wall. Knobbe fell to his knees. Hans cradled the old man in his arms. "It's me, Papa, truly. Hans. Your boy. I've come to set you free."

Knobbe turned away in shame. "Forgive me, lad. I wronged you."

"No wrongs, no wrongs." He stroked his father's hair.

"The things they asked me of your past," Knobbe whispered. "I know now who you are: A prince. My master. Oh, lad, I shall be your servant, forever and a day, if you'll have me."

Hans gazed tenderly into the grave robber's eyes. "I shall," he said, "but not as my servant. Rather, as my papa."

40

THE GREAT ESCAPE

Hans helped Knobbe to his feet. "We'll talk more, much more," he said. "But now we must flee."

"No need to tell me twice," Knobbe replied. "But there's someone else we must take with us."

"Who?"

On the other side of the corridor, a snore erupted as loud as a hog at market.

"Your friend's nurse," Knobbe quaked. "Wake her at your peril. There's no taming of the shrew!"

Hans followed the snore to its source. "Wake, Nurse, wake!"

Nurse roused with a start. "Vermin! Varlets!" She kicked and flailed as much as her chains would allow.

"I'm neither," Hans said. "I'm friend to Angela, who's alive and well beyond these walls."

Nurse blinked. "You're the Boy! Where have you come from, and how?"

"From the far mountains by avalanche and circus," he said, unlocking her shackles. "And you?"

"The soldiers caught me at my sister's and brought me here to be the dungeon master's wife. 'I'd rather marry a bucket of slop,' said I, for which he chained me to the wall."

"You know my father?" Hans asked.

"By smell only."

"Well, here he is in the flesh. Nurse, Knobbe; Knobbe, Nurse."

"Howdy-do," Nurse said, and hightailed it down the corridor. She braked at the sight of the Pandolinis' bears.

"*Ciao e buonasera,*" Pandolini beamed.

"These are friends, Nurse," Hans explained, as he and Knobbe caught up.

"If you say so." Nurse sniffed. "How do we get out of here?"

"At the end of the dungeon there's a lagoon that leads beyond the palace."

Knobbe blanched. "I can't swim."

"Neither can I," said Nurse.

"Nor any of us," Pandolini said with bravado. "But our bears can. They'll ferry us to safety."

Knobbe shook his head in terror. "Leave me here in the catacombs, the land of skulls and bones."

"Leave me as well," Nurse said.

"No," Hans said. "You're coming."

Nurse raised her fists. "Make me, boy. There's fight in me left."

Knobbe patted Hans on the back. "Never fear," he said. "I know my way around a graveyard. As for the dame, I'll keep her safe at my side."

Nurse squared her shoulders. "Yet keep your hands to yourself, and your eyes too, or there'll be a reckoning."

"Never fear," Knobbe cowered. He squeezed Hans' shoulders. "Now, truly, you must flee, and quickly too."

Hans hesitated, but knew the grave robber was right: Knobbe and Nurse would never dare the water or the bears, and further delay meant death. Hans handed him the executioner's hood, chain mail, pants, and boots. "Disguise yourself in these. The catacombs connect the dungeon to the cathedral. You can escape from there at night. Nurse can play your prisoner."

Pandolini twirled his hand anxiously. *"Arrivederci, arrivederci."*

"Sì. Arrivederci," Signora Pandolini echoed. She prodded the bears to the lagoon.

Hans embraced the grave robber one last time. "Fare thee well."

"Likewise," Knobbe said. "If ever I can do a favor, 'twould be an honor."

Hans' eyes lit up with inspiration. "As a matter of fact, you *can*. The Necromancer has announced three prophecies from the spirit world. You can help me break their power over the people."

"How?"

A tumult was descending from above. Hans whispered frantically in the old man's ear.

"I'll do it," the grave robber said. He and Nurse scuttled into the catacombs as Hans ran to the lagoon.

The bears had already lumbered into the water, Pandolini riding Balthazar, Signora Pandolini aboard Bianca. Hans hopped onto Bruno. *"Nuotate!"* Pandolini commanded, and the bears began to swim. No sooner had they turned a bend in the lagoon than Arnulf and his men stormed into the dungeon. Hans heard the archduke raging in the distance, then all was still, save for the water lapping the grotto's walls and the whoosh of bats above their heads.

The bears ferried them through the darkness as through a dreamless sleep. At last, flickers of light rippled over the water. A walkway rose on either side of the channel. The open bay was near.

Relief turned to horror. An iron grate blocked the exit. Chain pulleys ran up to wheels embedded in the high rock ceiling and looped back down onto hooks on the walkway walls. No wonder guards were only stationed at the front and rear palace gates. Who could raise such a barrier?

Pandolini smiled at the bears. "Ah, you, the strongest of my babes."

The bears snorted.

Hans and Bruno sloshed their way onto the walkway to the left, and Bianca and Pandolini to that on the right, while Balthazar kept the good *signora* afloat. The chains were swiftly unhooked from the wall and the bears harnessed.

"*Tirate, miei cari!*" Pandolini encouraged them.

Bruno and Bianca struggled down the walkways. The mighty grate began to rise. Soon it grazed the waterline.

"Best to hook the chains here to mask our escape," Hans told Pandolini. "Our friends can swim us underneath."

And so they did. Hidden by the mists that rose from the lagoon and the bushes that lined the bay, Hans, the bears, and the Pandolinis crawled onto the muddy bank some distance from the palace. The night air was alive with the peeps and trills of crickets and bullfrogs.

"Now to our *bambini*," Signora Pandolini said. "I hope your friend has kept them safe."

"Rest easy," Hans said. "Angela will have them hidden

in the forest where we planned. Nothing can go wrong."

The Pandolinis turned around three times and spat over their shoulders. Whenever anyone said nothing could go wrong, it always did.

ACT V

Johannes, Prince of Waldland

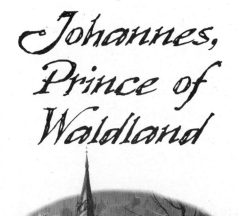

41
THE LUNATIC ASYLUM

*A*ngela led the Pandolini children through the fog to the rendezvous, a secluded clearing on the fringes of the great forest, a half mile east of the lunatic asylum. Without pausing for breath, she put Maria and Giuseppe in charge of their younger siblings, and set off to rescue her parents.

It was an easy job trekking though the huddle of houses between the forest and the asylum. Each shack swam into view, lit by the glow of the moon and the flames in the earthen pits before each door. But Angela grew frightened when these gave way to the wasteland around Asylum Hill. All she could see was the dreaded tower silhouetted against the mist; all she could hear, the ravings of its madmen; all she could smell, the stench of its dung heaps.

Angela got into character. She dirtied her face, adjusted the sash of her swashbuckler's costume, and set her broad-brimmed hat at a rakish angle. Next, she scratched herself and imagined manly thoughts. With a prayer to the god of happy endings, she swaggered up to the asylum's forbidding oak door, determined to play the brashest of daring young men.

The clapper was a gargoyle's head. Angela took it by the open mouth and banged three times. The booms of the bronze jaws silenced the cries within.

The window grate scraped open. "Who goes there?"

"A hired man come in service of Arnulf, Archduke of Waldland," Angela said with grim authority. "I'd speak with the keeper."

"Would you indeed." A pause. "Show your papers."

"I am about such deeds as need no papers," Angela declared. "Open this gate and bring me the keeper. Step lively too, if you wish to wake upon the morrow."

There was a heavy grunting and rattling of keys; the door creaked open. A man peered out. Hard and grizzled, he wore a dirty smock, fouled and glistening. Hair sprouted from his collar and cuffs, spreading up his neck and over the backs of his hands. Behind him, three grubby attendants held restraints and harnesses.

"I am the keeper," the man said. "What is the arch-duke's command?"

"He has sent me to take the Count and Countess von Schwanenberg to the dung heaps, there to slit their throats."

The keeper stared at her. "A moment." He closed the door. Angela heard loud muttering as he conferred with his attendants. The keeper reopened the door. "Enter," he said. "I'll lead you to the prisoners. You can save yourself trouble by killing them in their cell. After, my attendants will drag the bodies to the basement for dissection and disposal."

"I am grateful for your hospitality, but the archduke's instructions are clear. I am the one to do the deed, and on the dung heaps."

"As you wish," the keeper shrugged and let her in. Angela tried not to faint in the putrid air.

The keeper took a torch from the wall and led her up the winding tower stairs. Endless cells emerged from the dark as from a nightmare. Gnarly hands flew between the bars at Angela's face. She held a hand to her hat, lest a lunatic grab its brim and tear off her disguise.

At last, they reached the top of the tower.

"The Count and Countess," the keeper sneered. He opened the peephole in an iron door. "The archduke's kept them chained in their finery. Oh, how they struggled when they arrived. They're not so high and mighty now."

Angela peeked through the spy hole. Moonlight shone through slits on the outer wall. She saw her father in shadow, his hands manacled to a beam above his head. Her mother was slumped forward on a stool, her foot cuffed in a leg iron. Angela recognized the back of her wig, and the funeral dress she'd worn on the day of the burial. She struggled not to weep.

The keeper unlocked the door and handed her the key to her parents' locks. Angela flew to her mother, dropped to her knees, and felt for the ankle cuff. "Mother," she whispered, "it's me. Angela. I've come to bring you home."

"My darling girl." Her mother caressed her shoulders.

Angela froze. The voice and touch were strange. She looked up slowly—into the hollow eye sockets of the Necromancer.

"Did you miss me?" the Necromancer purred.

Angela screamed. "Father!" The man hanging from the chains swung around—a lunatic with a lantern jaw and bugged eyes. "Dolly, my dolly!" he leered.

The Necromancer clutched Angela with his bony claws. "I knew you'd come, my sweet. Ah, the love of a child for its parents." The keeper's assistants swarmed Angela. "Life may be more fantastic than stories," the Necromancer continued. "Still, didn't you wonder how you entered the madhouse so easily?"

The keeper put a hood over Angela's head. The

Necromancer cinched it tight. "At midday tomorrow, you and your parents will be taken to Market Square to burn as witches," he gloated. "Your fate will lure the grave robber's apprentice, and the two of you will roast together."

*H*ans led Signor and Signora Pandolini through the shantytown by the harbor. They navigated its alleys with ease: Snitches were unknown here, and even the most brutish louts ran in terror from the bears. Hans spirited them from the slums into the forest, and soon they approached the rendezvous.

The moon hung heavy. At times it shone a path through the canopy; at others, its light disappeared in fog. A thick bank of mist rolled in. The bears stopped in their tracks; the hair on their necks rose; their heads hunched into their shoulders. The Pandolinis crouched beside them. "What is it?" Pandolini whispered into Balthazar's ear.

Balthazar replied with a low growl. Hans felt the presence, too: eyes that circled them in the dark.

"Who's there?" he called out. Without warning, there was a bounding in the night. Something pounced out of the fog, knocked Hans to the ground, and vanished. Hans scrambled to his knees. The attacker struck again. It hit his knees from the left and toppled him from the right. Other creatures leaped about him. He felt a hot breath at his throat. He flailed wildly.

"Run," Hans called to the Pandolinis. "Take the bears and save your children."

A monstrous tongue licked his face. Hans thought of Angela and prepared to die. Instead, the fog rolled through and Hans stared his attacker in the eye.

"Siegfried!" he shouted in delight.

The great wolf wagged its tail. The rest of the pack frolicked in the mist.

"What's happening?" Pandolini trembled.

"These are old friends," Hans exclaimed. "The pack of the Wolf King. He and his men must be nearby." He scratched Siegfried's ears. The wolf rolled its head in ecstasy. Hans rose and clapped his hand to his thigh. "Siegfried, Angela is with my friends' children in a nearby clearing. Come with us to greet them, then lead us to your master."

As if understanding, Siegfried and the pack accompanied Hans and the Pandolinis to the meeting place. But instead of children, they found the Wolf King and his crew tied up with silk scarves.

"Tomas Bundt," Hans exclaimed. He quickly freed him.

"Hans!" Tomas' Adam's apple nearly popped out of his mouth.

"Mamma, Papà," peeped a chorus of tiny voices from the treetops.

Signora Pandolini threw open her arms. *"Bambini!"*

The children pointed at the wolves and wailed.

Pandolini nervously patted Siegfried's head. *"Amici, bambini."*

The Pandolini children scampered down the trees and hugged their parents.

"The little devils were in the branches," Tomas said, helping Hans untie his comrades. "When the wolves ran off, they dropped down, bound several of us in an instant, and returned to the treetops to ambush the next of our number." He blushed. "Don't tell a soul. We have our reputations to think of."

"Your secret's safe," Hans smiled. "But where's Angela?"

"Nearby, I hope. The hermits have taken our horses to look for her."

Hans was thunderstruck. "The hermits are here too?"

Tomas nodded. "We were camped near the mountain when we heard the avalanche. From the tree line, we saw them flying down the slopes in coffins and went to help them. They had your old monk's robe. Siegfried used the scent to find the circus camp. From there we followed the wagon tracks, catching up as you reached the city. We stashed our gear and ringed the palace, keeping to the shadows. Tonight, we saw the children escape from the turret. We followed their trail here. You and Angela were missing. But there was a path heading west—"

"West?" Hans gasped. "That's the asylum. Angela—"

"With luck, the hermits will stop her before she gets there," Tomas said.

As if on cue, the hermits entered the clearing. Their beards and hair were trimmed and their robes exchanged for the tunics and breeches that had been packed in the mountain cave. Though physically unrecognizable, their bearing was unmistakable: solid and graceful, with a quiet strength that spoke of courage.

"The lad's safe," Tomas called out.

A tall, broad-shouldered man bounded forward and hoisted Hans in the air. "My boy," he whooped, "I made you a promise: 'Wherever you are, fear not, for I am with you. I've lost you once and never shall again.' Now, by my troth, I make good my word!"

"Father," Hans exclaimed. "Or should I call you Archduke Fredrick?"

"So, you know the truth at last!" Fredrick laughed. "You're as bright as you are bold." He set Hans down.

"Call me Father, Son, and know your true name as well: Johannes, Prince of Waldland." He turned Hans to face the others. "Behold, this is my belovèd son, in whom I am well pleased."

The men dropped on one knee and placed their hands over their hearts. "Long live Johannes, Prince of Waldland."

The Pandolinis burst into applause. The bears rose on their hind legs and twirled in a circle.

"*Magnifico!*" Pandolini cheered. "Had you put this on a stage, I should scarce have believed it!"

"But what about Angela?" Hans asked. "Did you find her?"

There was a terrible silence.

"We saw her enter the asylum tower," Fredrick said. "Immediately, soldiers hiding behind the dung heaps surrounded it. She's trapped."

"We must free her," Hans said, "and restore you to the throne."

"A wonderful dream, but how?" asked one of the hermits. "Arnulf has an army, we are but few."

"We'll rally the archduchy," Hans replied.

"Who'll fight for a ruler they think is dead?" Tomas frowned.

"And what of the prophecies?" Pandolini quivered. "They say Arnulf will reign forever. Who'll brave the spirit world?"

"I, for one," said Hans boldly. "I welcome the challenge to defeat the tyrant, his necromancer, and all the forces at their command."

"Spoken like a true prince of Waldland," his father beamed.

"How shall we proceed?" the men asked.

"I've a plan to fulfill the prophecies," Hans said. "If we defeat their power, the people will have the courage to join our side."

The men leaned in. "What's your plan?"

Hans held their gaze with a look of fierce determination. "First," he said. . . .

43

HIGH STAKES

*A*ll morning, town criers heralded the news that Angela and her parents were to be burned at the stake for witchcraft. As the people readied themselves, Knobbe was hard at work at the task Hans had given him.

"You know the memorial pillar in Market Square?" Hans had whispered before escaping through the lagoon. "The entrance to the foundation is in the catacombs. I need you to climb up the inside and chisel the bottom out of one of the memorial coffins. Then, follow the catacombs to the door leading up to the cathedral. I'll meet you there, midday tomorrow."

Knobbe would've acted at once, but Arnulf had arrived and he and Nurse had had to hide all night on a shelf of bones while the archduke's new dungeon master had a training session on the old. When Arnulf left at dawn, they'd crawled from hiding as the new dungeon master was hauling his predecessor's carcass to the lime pit. Nurse had whacked him silly with a thighbone. "Is he dead?" she'd asked. "No such luck," Knobbe'd sighed. "Take his uniform. We'll stuff him in a bone barrel, gagged with a dead rat."

The delay meant that Nurse now had her own executioner's disguise. But it also meant that Knobbe had only begun to hack the bottom from the pillar coffin with a chisel he'd taken from the dungeon.

"Quickly," Nurse said, her bosom testing her new chain mail tunic.

Chunks of marble fell from the darkness and landed by her feet.

"By all the saints, woman, I'm hacking as fast as I can."

A voice echoed along the passageway. "Dungeon master?" It was Arnulf.

Meanwhile, Hans and his father, Fredrick, were entering the city dressed in cloaks, tunics, and broad-brimmed hats from the hermitage trunks. Soon they were swept up in a surging crowd, the streets swelling like rivers, as citizens poured from their homes to the witch burning. The crowd flooded into Market Square.

The first thing Hans saw were three mountainous piles of wood, guarded by a four-ring cordon of soldiers. Each of the stacks towered twenty feet in the air and was topped by a ten-foot stake. How could they get to Angela and her parents? Even harder, how could they escape with them through the soldiers and crowd?

Hans waited until his father was in position near the reviewing stand in front of the palace. Then he slipped into the cathedral and darted through the shadows of the nave to the pipe organ. Behind was the barred door that opened onto the stairwell to the catacombs. An old friend disguised in executioner's gear was waiting for him.

"Here as planned." Hans smiled at his other papa.

"Not exactly as planned," said Nurse, raising her hood. "Your Knobbe was called away by the archduke."

Back in the forest, the Pandolini children limbered up for a grand performance, while the hermits retrieved the swords and bucklers they'd stowed in the hollowed tree trunks near the city's edge. Those who'd joined the hermitage from nearby counties had spent the night galloping on the Wolf King's horses to their former estates. Trusted neighbors, families, servants, and friends had returned with them to make a stand for their rightful ruler, Archduke Fredrick. It was a noble sight: a hundred stout hearts and a circus family prepared to throw themselves against the might of Arnulf's army.

Tomas addressed the crowd. "For our fight to succeed, we must fulfill the three prophecies. Hans—the prince Johannes—has given us a plan. Its cunning shall inspire legends and plays."

Tomas was interrupted by a rumbling beyond the trees. A carriage flanked by cavalry thundered down the hill from the asylum. The Necromancer was crouched beside the coachman, whipping the horses with abandon.

"They're taking Angela and her parents to execution," Tomas cried. "Do as Hans ordered! Chop down the leafiest bushes and saplings you can find!"

TWO PROPHECIES FULFILLED

*T*he carriage stopped at the center of Market Square.
The Necromancer opened the door for Angela and
her parents and bowed in mockery. A hush fell over the
crowd as he escorted them through the cordon of soldiers
to the wooden stacks, lumps of coal bulging from his eye
sockets.

The base of each pile was swathed in oily rags. In front,
a torch pole the length of a longstaff was mounted in a heavy
brass holder next to a flaming cauldron. The executioner
hunched beside it in a black hood, chain mail tunic, black
leather trousers, and boots. His assistants, the dungeon
twins, clapped their hands and giggled.

Angela steadied herself. She turned to her mother and father. "I love you," she said simply.

"And we, you." Her mother buried her head in the count's shoulder. The twins pulled them apart and yanked them up the outer piles of wood.

Angela took a deep breath and extended her hand to the executioner as gallantly as a heroine of legend. He led her up the center stack. While he bound her to the stake, Angela held back her terror by imagining happy endings. None seemed possible until the executioner leaned in to her ear and whispered, "Take heart, girlie. Hans is near."

In that instant, Angela noticed that the executioner's right shoulder was the size of a small pumpkin. "It can't be. Are you . . . ?" But he'd already turned and shambled back to his torch pole.

The Necromancer raised a voice trumpet. "Today we shall rejoice in the death of three notorious witches," he announced, "creatures who have conspired with warlocks against our great ruler, Arnulf, Archduke of Waldland."

There were a few cries of, "Death to the witches," but for the most part, silence. The pitiable sight of Angela and her parents had turned all but the heartiest witch burners mute.

The Necromancer popped the coals from his sockets and tossed them in the air. With uncanny aim, they landed in the cauldron. On cue, buglers on a palace parapet played the royal fanfare. All eyes turned to the reviewing stand. The archbishop, generals, counselors, chief stewards, sundry magistrates and county overseers rose as one. Arnulf appeared under the black velvet canopy of his private box to the applause of his soldiers.

"Long live Arnulf, Archduke of Waldland," cheered the Necromancer.

The crowd mumbled a refrain and fell to its knees. Except one man.

Tall and broad-shouldered, with a ruddy face, trim white beard, and eyes so blue they dazzled the sun, the stranger jutted his chin at the archduke. "Villain! Tyrant!" his voice rang out, as crisp and clear as a mountain spring. "Today, you and your wizard would burn three innocents at the stake. Their crime? To shield the life and virtue of a maiden you sought to defile."

The air trembled. Not even the bravest soldiers dared blink.

Arnulf's lips turned a violent purple. "Who are you, miscreant?"

"One who counted you my brother, but knows you as the devil himself," the man replied. He doffed his hat. "Yes, Arnulf! It is I, Fredrick, rightful archduke of Waldland, whose death you sought, and that of my child, to steal the crown."

Citizens struggled for a glimpse of the stranger—the

elder remembering the glory times of the good archduke, the younger to see the man whom their parents praised behind locked doors.

Sweat trickled down Arnulf's neck. But what is truth next to a lie believed? He pointed to the memorial pillar. "Madman," he scoffed. "Behold the coffins of my brother and his boy."

"Empty," Fredrick said, "for I am alive, and so is my son and heir."

"Guards," Arnulf ordered. "Arrest the lunatic and tie him to the stake beside the girl."

Before anyone could move, there was a frantic trumpeting. Sentries from the city's edge galloped into the square, scattering citizens in all directions.

"The great forest!" they cried.

"What about the great forest?" Arnulf thundered.

"We looked to the mist that lingers at the forest's edge," the first declared. "We saw trees and bushes rise from the ground—rise from the ground and march!"

"What?"

"The prophecy's come true," the second exclaimed. "The great forest is marching on the capital! With it, wolves and a host of otherworldly beasts—creatures with necks so tall they graze the sky! Sure 'tis the Wolf King and his monster horde."

Gasps rose from the crowd.

"Quickly, men, the mirrored shields!" Arnulf shrieked.

Some of the soldiers ran to the armory; others spun in circles.

The Necromancer held the rest in check: "Two prophecies remain that shield the archduke better than any mirror," he hollered into his voice trumpet. "His Royal Highness shall reign till an eagle rises from stone, and his severed hands sail over a sea of bones."

At those words, there was a grating sound at the top of the pillar. The lid of the smallest stone coffin toppled over and smashed into pieces. Eyes widened as Hans squeezed up through the hole that Knobbe had chiseled in its bottom. "Behold!" Hans cried, and bared the eagle birthmark on his right shoulder.

"Arnulf, your time has come," Angela shouted from her pyre. "An eagle has risen from stone."

Market Square rocked in shock.

Arnulf's face bleached, stiff as starch. "The second prophecy may be fulfilled, yet I have a third to protect me." He raised the golden reliquary slung around his neck. "Never shall these severed hands sail over a sea of bones!"

With that, he sprang from his box, wielding his sword. In a flurry of leaps, he was at the pillar, bounding up its steps. Soldiers blocked the stairs against any who'd come to Hans' defense.

Hans squeezed back down the coffin hole. Arnulf

smashed it wide with an iron fist. "Now, brother, I go to slice your brat in two," the monster exulted. "Guards! Seize him!"

Soldiers circled Fredrick as Arnulf jumped down the hole after Hans. But citizens around Fredrick rose from their knees. Other soldiers, too, cast their lot with their rightful ruler. A riot broke out. The cordon of guards around the witch stakes weakened.

"There's no time to wait," the Necromancer screamed at the executioner. "Light the bonfires!"

"Only if you be on the pyre," the executioner replied.

The Necromancer froze. "That voice!"

"Yes, 'tis I, Knobbe the Bent," the grave robber laughed, and tore off his executioner's hood. "Did the stink of the crowd and them catacomb bones dull the scent of our county swamps?"

In a rage, the Necromancer grabbed the flaming cauldron with both hands. His palms sizzled as he tossed it to its side. Fiery coals bounced across the cobblestones onto the oily rags below Angela. At once, fire engulfed the base of her wooden hill.

"Help!" Angela cried, but the crowd retreated in terror from the blaze—as creatures on horseback galloped into the square. With the sentries fled, the Wolf King's men had stormed the capital—the Pandolini children clinging to their backs, the wolf pack racing at their heels. The wolves dashed everywhere. Panicked citizens fled to the parapets, toppling soldiers over balustrades.

The fire roared higher. Angela screamed to the Wolf King. He spurred his men to the bonfire. Their horses reared, unable to leap above the flames.

Amid the pandemonium, the Necromancer fled beneath the reviewing stand. Fearful of the mob, he hid under swaths of bunting and pulled a vial of sleeping potion from his shroud. *One whiff of this, and I'll appear dead*, he cackled to himself. *Come night, I'll rise and escape into the dark.*

The soldiers seizing Fredrick succumbed to the crowd. He broke free and turned to help Hans. But Angela's screams tore his heart. He ran to the pyre, where the Pandolinis had formed a human pyramid. Maria'd tied one end of the silk rope to the torch pole and scampered up the pyramid with the other. Knowing exactly what to do, Fredrick grabbed the pole like a longstaff and vaulted onto Tomas' saddle, where he braced it in a stirrup.

Maria bent her knees and somersaulted from the top of the human pyramid to the top of Angela's woodpile. She loosed Angela's bonds and tied the silk rope to the stake. Taut above the flames, it ran like a high wire to the long-staff.

Maria slid hand over hand to safety. Angela clutched the rope, swung her legs high, and found the line with her ankles. She wriggled along the rope. The blaze exploded behind her. The rope burned through and she swung to the ground at the foot of Fredrick's pole, and into the loving embrace of her parents, already freed by Knobbe.

"Now to my son!" Fredrick exclaimed. But he couldn't move. The cheering throng swept him onto their shoulders, his cries for Hans lost in their roars.

Siegfried scared a path through the crowd to Angela. She zipped down the opening. As it closed in the crush, Angela slipped between legs and under arms, clawing and biting her final steps to the cathedral. Inside, she barreled through the nave and nipped behind the organ.

The stairs to the cellar were guarded by an executioner. Angela held her breath. Nurse raised her hood.

"Nurse! You! How?" Angela exclaimed.

"Don't ask."

Roars echoed up from below.

"It's Hans and the archduke," Nurse said. "Who knows how long the lad can survive!"

Angela dived into the catacombs.

45

A FIGHT TO THE DEATH

When Hans had scurried down inside the pillar five minutes earlier, he had had no idea what to do next. In stories, prophecies always came in threes, but Hans had hoped that in real life having the great forest march on the capital and an eagle rise out of stone would be enough to overthrow Arnulf. Apparently not. He'd have to make the archduke's severed hands sail over a sea of bones. But how?

Above, the archduke had broken a bigger opening in the stone coffin and was charging down the pillar.

Hans ran toward the dungeon in search of a weapon. Walls of bones rose above him. He skirted the catacomb lime pit, sprinted past the skeletons on the wall of the central passageway, and burst into the dungeon cavern.

"Come out, come out, wherever you are," the archduke taunted from behind.

Should he hide? No. That might do for a grave robber's apprentice, but not for a prince of Waldland. He ran to the fire pit and seized a red-hot poker.

"So there you are," came a low purr.

Hans whirled around. Arnulf was framed in the archway.

The villain unleashed a hideous grin. "You're trapped."

"We'll see," Hans said, and waved the poker.

"It wants to live, does it?" Arnulf advanced, swinging his broadsword like a scythe. Hans moved backward to the left; Arnulf countered. Hans moved backward to the right; Arnulf countered again.

"You and your father love the people," Arnulf spat. "Fie on you. The world works on fear, not kindness. Leave goodness to fairy tales."

Hans imagined the hermitage pell. He charged at Arnulf with a roar. Arnulf blocked the strike and sent Hans reeling backward to the wall.

"Here's how *iron hands* strike a pell," Arnulf mocked. He brandished his sword over his head and ran at Hans, swinging hard. Hans dropped and rolled to the side. Arnulf's sword clanged on the rock face. Hans jabbed Arnulf's thigh with the red-hot poker. Arnulf howled and punched a fist at the ground. He hit the poker; it broke at the handle.

Hans leaped up. Arnulf diced the air with his sword. Hans dodged, grabbed a torch from the wall, and ran to the torture rack. He slid underneath. The archduke followed.

Hans turned and shoved the torch in Arnulf's face. His greasy hair burst into flames. Arnulf pushed himself out from under the rack, and spun to the lagoon to douse the fire. It was too far to run. In panic, he stuck his head in the dungeon poop bucket.

Hans laughed and scrambled up the pulleys of the torture rack to the rafters.

"You'll pay for this," Arnulf screamed through a haze of steaming pee. He raised his sword to sever the ropes and send Hans toppling—but a shrill eagle's cry filled the dungeon.

Arnulf whirled around. He saw the shadow of a giant bird. It flared its wings and flew across the cavern walls.

Arnulf shivered, then spotted Angela hiding in a rock crevice by a torch. "Why, it's a shadow puppet!" he sneered. "You're here to die too, are you, girl?"

"No. To see the third prophecy fulfilled!" she tossed back.

"Arnulf!" Hans called from above.

Arnulf looked up and around. Hans was holding an iron pulley weight. He pitched it at the archduke's head. It made a direct hit.

The archduke doubled over in pain. The reliquary box

on the gold chain around his neck swung back and forth.

Hans grabbed a hooked rope. He tossed it through the loop of the swinging chain and yanked. The hook caught the chain and broke it; the reliquary box crashed across the floor.

Hans swung from the rafters on the rope. His heels hit the archduke square in the jaw. Arnulf fell to his knees.

Hans scooted for the reliquary box. He snapped the catch and grabbed the severed hands.

"Unhand my bones!" Arnulf hollered.

"Run!" Hans called to Angela. They barreled down the corridor into the catacombs, Arnulf in pursuit. At the lime pit, they split down separate alleys. Arnulf ran to the end of the widening. "The only exit leads by me," he crowed.

He saw the shadow of a wolf on a wall of bones. "Ah, the girl who cried wolf," he laughed. "I've seen your puppet tricks before." A low growl. "I've heard your vocal tricks too."

Hans popped from an alley. "But this is no trick. Is it, Siegfried?"

The great wolf appeared. Arnulf swung his sword. The blade shattered against a wall support.

Hans held up the hand bones, clasped in a mockery of prayer. "Fetch!" he cried, and threw them into the air above the lime pit.

Arnulf leaped at them blindly. But Siegfried leaped

farther and faster. He snatched the bones with his teeth and cleared the pit. Arnulf wasn't so lucky. He splashed face-first into the lime. He screeched to his feet, flesh bubbling.

Hans circled the pit. Arnulf raged right through it. He swung at Hans with his iron fists. They hit the wall supports as Hans bobbed and weaved. The beams began to crack and splinter, their shelves to tilt.

"You can't escape me!" Arnulf yowled. "One strike is all I need." He wiped his forehead. It slid right off. "I'M MELTING!" he cried. He hammered the beam by Hans' head. His fist wedged in the split timber. He yanked it out. There was a terrible sound, like a ship breaking apart at sea.

The beam buckled. So did the beams around it. Shelves tipped over, spilling their walls of bones in torrential waves. Arnulf was caught in a swell. Arm bones pulled him under. Leg bones held him fast.

Hans and Angela ran toward the cathedral cellar.

"Siegfried?" Hans called.

The great wolf frisked beyond the archduke.

Hans whistled. "Here, boy!"

Siegfried made a short bound and a mighty leap. In his powerful mouth, Arnulf's severed hands sailed over the sea of bones.

"I believe that's the third prophecy," Hans called over his shoulder.

Arnulf was drowning in skeletons. He tried to swim his way out. No use. The weight of the bones pinned him in the dark.

All around was scurry and squeak. Rats. Hundreds of rats crawling out of the catacomb skulls to feed.

46
JUST DESERTS

*S*inging and dancing continued into the night as Waldland's citizens reveled in the tyrant's fall and the restoration of Archduke Fredrick. Time alone could right the evils of Arnulf's reign, but for now Waldland celebrated the beginning of a beginning.

Under the reviewing stand, the Necromancer lay still as a corpse. The potion was wearing off slowly; though unable to move or speak, his mind had cleared. *If I can get out of the city, I can live underground to plot my revenge,* he thought. *But how to escape unseen when the streets are full of merrymakers?*

It was amid such fears that the Necromancer received

an unexpected visit. Two little creatures, the likes of which could hide in dustbins, crept into the shadows of the stand and lifted the bunting from his face.

"We see'd you come here, Master," said one. "We waited for you to come out all day. You's still asleeplike, ain't you?"

Are you my Weevils? the Necromancer wondered. *How did you escape the castle? Why did you come to the capital?*

The second Weevil read his mind. "You taughts us to hide where none would thinks to search for us," he said. "That's what we done. We hid by the palace where you'd never think to look."

"Yes, Master, it's like we got a cloak invisible. An' now we's come to spirit you from this place."

Oh, clever pets, how I misjudged you, the Necromancer thought. *There shall be treats indeed for stealing me from the city.*

Each of the Weevils took a leg and hauled the Necromancer into the square. Under the bunting, he looked like a pile of cloth. No one paid heed as they lugged him down the streets, his head bouncing on the cobblestones, nor as they dragged him onto the dirt road leading out of town.

The Necromancer tried to tell them to take care, that the sticks and stones that littered the way were piercing his flesh; but his lips were mute, his limbs limp.

Now the most terrible smell. *Ah, yes*—his mind smiled—*they're taking me to the dumping grounds. What crafty pets. It's the perfect place from which to plot my revenge.*

But the Weevils dragged him ever onward. Now upward. They stopped. The Necromancer heard the banging of a heavy door knocker and the sound of a window grate sliding open.

"What do you want?" It was the keeper's voice. They were at the asylum.

"We's got a rare treat worth a few pennies. Come, take a look at our prize."

The door creaked open. "What have we here?" the keeper said. "My, how the mighty have fallen."

"Him's dead. All fresh and all," the Weevils advised. "You'd best cuts him up 'fore he goes bad."

But I'm alive, the Necromancer tried to scream. *I'm alive.*

"I've always wanted to see inside that brain," the keeper said. "I'll get to work at once." He gave the Weevils a handful of coins and called his attendants to ready his knives and pickling jars.

No! the Necromancer howled silently. *I'm alive! I'M ALIVE!*

The keeper whistled a cheerful song, tossed the Necromancer over his shoulder, and carried him to the basement.

47

ALL'S WELL THAT ENDS WELL

*T*he palace windows were opened wide to clear the air. The harbor helped, sending a breeze that swept away the nightly fog for the first time in memory. In the banquet hall, the Pandolinis and their bears performed their finest circus ever under the light of a thousand lamps and candelabra.

Archduke Fredrick had ceded the seats of honor to Hans and Angela. They sat together at the center of the great table with all their friends and family. On Hans' right, his two fathers, Fredrick and Knobbe, chatted together with the former hermits. On his left, Angela reunited with her parents and Nurse in the company of Tomas and his fellows; Nurse moved to Knobbe's side sometime before dessert. Angela smiled: Nurse had a need to teach the social graces, and in Knobbe she'd have her most challenging pupil yet.

"You found my son, Johannes, and named him Hans," Fredrick said to Knobbe. "A different form of the same name."

Knobbe scratched his ear. "Sure, our names and deeds be written in the stars."

Fredrick smiled. "Or in our hopes and dreams."

A paw de trois from the dancing bears led to a standing ovation.

Fredrick rose and addressed the Pandolinis. "In gratitude for your service, remain as our privileged guests for as long as you desire."

"*Grazie.*" Pandolini bowed. "Yet we are wanted home to the court of Venice. The Doge has held concerns about his neighbor, Waldland, and will be pleased by our report that all is well."

Fredrick raised a friendly eyebrow. "You're close with the Doge?"

"People see what they expect," the showman winked. "Poor circus folk look alike to the world. We can come and go like hermits."

"Then give our best to your Venetian lord," Fredrick declared. "We shall send you safe by royal escort." He turned to Tomas. "As for you, Tomas Bundt, lawless high-wayman and thief . . ."

Tomas cowered.

"The archduchy is in your debt. A full pardon to you and your men."

Tomas was so relieved he fell back against his friends.

"Stand tall," Fredrick ordered. "Our new poet laureate and his court musicians must have their heads high above the clouds."

"Poet laureate?" Tomas hopped to his feet in disbelief.

"Court musicians?" chorused his men.

"Indeed," Hans said. "Who but an Artist and Poet Extraordinaire can pen the sagas of our land? And who better to set those poems to song?"

With a great cheer, Tomas was hoisted high.

The archduke's eyes fell next on the grave robber. He drew his sword. "On your knees."

Knobbe dropped to the floor in terror.

Fredrick placed the blade on Knobbe's right shoulder. "Who but a plucky grave robber should guard the royal catacombs?" he asked. "Rise and henceforth be known as Sir Knobbe the Bent, Keeper of the Crypt."

Knobbe forgot himself. He bounced to his feet in joy, planted a kiss on the archduke's cheek, hugged Hans, and took Nurse for a spin around the room to applause and laughter.

"There's yet one thing you've forgotten, Father," Hans said. "Our land has suffered under the weight of what *is*. We need a glimpse of what *might be*. I propose that a court theater be built where we can see our stories on the stage, and imagine better endings than have ever been."

"And who should run this theater?" Fredrick asked.

Hans turned to Angela. "Only the finest, bravest soul in the whole archduchy. The Countess Angela Gabriela von Schwanenberg: the first who dared to challenge the usurper; who risked her life to save her parents; and in whose service, and by whose light, I grew to be your son."

Angela blushed.

Fredrick turned to the count and countess. "Has Angela your blessing to live at court?"

They hesitated.

Angela rolled her eyes. "Oh for heaven's sake, it's not as if I can get into any more mischief than I already have."

"True," her parents laughed. "With Nurse as your chaperone, we're agreed."

The hall erupted in revelry. Hans and Angela slipped out onto a balcony to enjoy the night sky. The young prince glanced shyly at Angela. "It's been a grand adventure."

"Indeed," she teased. "You've done quite well for a servant."

"And you for a witch," he teased back. He took her hand. They gazed at the heavens.

Angela rested her head on his shoulder. "I love happy endings," she sighed.

"Then just for you," Hans smiled, "I'll take my cue and say, 'The End.'"

ACKNOWLEDGMENTS

When I was a kid, my mom took me to every play at the Stratford Shakespeare Festival. My first was *Twelfth Night* when I was five. The spectacle got me—actors running on stage from all directions with brandished swords and swirling banners. Soon, though, it was the stories: magnificent tales of families separated by the sea and reunited; of evil, usurping dukes; of witches, star-crossed lovers, and bold comic characters with names like Sir Toby Belch and Justice Shallow. I was hooked by worlds of wonder in which the confusions of my young life found voice.

I couldn't get enough. When I wasn't seeing the plays, I

was reading the stories as told by Classics Illustrated Comics and Charles and Mary Lamb. In my teens, I did summer jobs at the festival: as an usher, a dresser, and finally as an acting apprentice. I remember barreling across Stratford's thrust stage as an Albany soldier, cowering before Lear's rage as a Goneril servant, and actually delivering a speech as one of Duke Senior's banished lords in the Forest of Arden.

Family and friends; secrets and identity; transformation and reconciliation—these are the themes I've held close to my heart since I was a child and that find expression in this tale. So, above all else, I want to thank my mother, the most courageous, inspiring person I know, who introduced me to the magic and power of words and the way in which Story can give shape and meaning to life's chaos.

I also want to thank Daniel Legault, Louise and Christine Baldacchino, Sebastien Amenta, Mark Citro, and David Stone, who read and critiqued the manuscript throughout its many drafts.

Last but not least, I'd like to thank everyone at HarperCollins for the tussles that wrestled this book into being—especially Lynne Missen, Sarah Sevier, Catherine Onder, Susan Rich, Kathryn Hinds, Tyler Infinger, Jessica Berg, Alison Klapthor, and Hadley Dyer. And, of course, Beth Fleisher, Joe Monti, and Barry Goldblatt at Barry Goldblatt Literary.

—Allan Stratton

All the world's a stage,
And all the men and women merely players.
They have their exits and their entrances,
And one man in his time plays many parts.

—William Shakespeare, *As You Like It*